Offensive
Behavior

ANDREW P. COHEN
with K.L SILVA and R.L. CANTRELL

ISBN: 0990667618
ISBN-13: 978-0990667612

DEDICATION

In no particular order, I would like to thank & acknowledge the people who were teammates, family & friends, some of them who pulled my chestnuts out of the fire more than once. For privacy purposes, I will not mention real names, but those who were there, know who they are & I thank you.

While I was out saving my clients and their little piece of the world it was my kids who sacrificed the most, I missed out on a lot with them. I want them to know how much I love them, Ashli & Aaron you guys are my world!

Julie, thanks and I'm sorry for the sleepless nights.

To my "brother" Pepper my kids still have a father thanks to you, I love you man!

Robin, over a decade! Yeah yeah, fuck me runnin I know. Thanks for everything. Really.

Kerri, thanks for sharing me with your friends & family, it's nice to have an East Coast support group.

"Teddy" - R.I.P. I'll never forget what you taught me. "nobody gets left behind" Thank you for bringing me home you carried me and now I carry you everyday. HOOYAH!

To my teammates: I learned a lot, saw a lot & used it all. Our "dirty dozen" was a brotherhood, I didn't understand what that really meant until you taught me that real heroes don't wear capes, they wear combat boots and carry their brothers home when they can't do it themselves. Thanks for the opportunities, the teachings & the life lessons, there isn't a day that goes by I don't use them.

Kristen, what say we take a "vacation" huh? No beaches, NO WATER? I love you babe.

To all of those who get dressed every morning knowing you're going into harms way for others...keep low, don't cast a shadow & come home to those who love you. Thank You All!

Arielle, you have no idea how much I miss you everyday, you can come home at anytime you like.

THE BODYGUARD

TRANSIENT FACES WITH NO NAMES,

I GET PAID TO TAKE THE BULLET OR THE BLADE.

TIMES ARE TOUGH, THINGS ARE HARD, THIS IS MY CALLING CARD.

I'M THE BODYGUARD.

I GET PAID TO GET YOU THROUGH LIFE, WHILE SOMEONE OUT THERE

TRIES TO GET YOU WITH A KNIFE.

SNIPERS ON THE ROOF, YOU'RE UNDER FIRE, DONT WORRY SIR,

MY SKILLS ARE FOR HIRE.

I AM THE BODYGUARD.

SHOTGUNS, H&K'S, GLOCK WEAPONS TOO, ALL THE WHILE YOU'RE SLEEPING,

I'LL BE WATCHING OVER YOU.

I'LL KEEP YOU ALIVE, JUST DO WHAT I SAY.

I KNOW THIS BUSINESS WELL AND DEAD CLIENTS DONT PAY.

I AM YOU'RE BODYGUARD!

THIS WAS WRITTEN BY A. COHEN IN 1993
1050 HRS. AFTER A HOME INVASION ON A CLIENT IN SOUTHERN
CALIFORNIA AFTER SPENDING A QUIET EVENING WATCHING
OVER A FAMILY OF FOUR.

(GOOD GUY 3 / BAD GUYS 0)

CONTENTS

CHAPTER 1
REFELCTIONS 1989

The whine of the twin engines had barely ceased, when the door to the Learjet opened and the steps lowered to touch the dirt floor of the private hangar. A large figure appeared in the doorway, methodically scanning the area with a well-seasoned eye.

Ever so gingerly, cautiously, he took each step, one after the other until he reached the ground. Crouching, the man searched under the plane, hoping to find nothing. As he turned into the light that seeped through the double bay doors, anyone who may have been in close proximity would see the H & K MP5 submachine gun cradled in his arms, matching every move he made.

When satisfied the area was secure, he pulled a small transmitter from a belt holster and spoke into it, "All clear sir."

The second man to exit the plane was similar to the first, although he was wearing something other than BDU's (battle dress uniform). Upon closer inspection however, there were certain things that would give him away as a member of the protective detail. One such thing, the combat boots he wore with his Nino Cerutti, double breasted, steel-blue, pinstriped suit.

The man who tailored this outfit was a master. Much thought and attention to detail goes into tailoring a suit for a man this size. For a man who carries so much hardware, yet goes undetected, a suit such as this is as important to him as his weaponry. Sporting a flattop haircut, showed another telltale sign this man was not who he seemed. As far as Terrence Calhoun was concerned, no one could cut his hair like himself.

Looking over at his partner Jason, Terry thought back on how they had been working together for five years this month. Promises to Jason and his wife Amanda, to dinner for a dual celebration when this assignment was over, played in Terry's mind. Two anniversaries were to be toasted: one, the wedding anniversary of Jason and his bride, the other, of Terry and Jason's partnership. Thoughts of steak and champagne brought a brief smile, with the anticipation of the feast they would share in about 72-hours.

Rounding the front of the plane, Terry watched the third member of the detail come down the stairs with an older man, the POTC (President of the Corporation). Ponce was the newest guy on the team. While working for a couple that hired Terry and Jason for a private party, Terry had the opportunity to meet Ponce.

Escorting an elderly gentleman, who really didn't need a bodyguard, Ponce was more of a companion who could keep the street vermin away. Watching him all night, Jason and Terry were impressed with his professionalism. As Ponce was about to leave the party, Jason handed him a card asking him to call if he was interested in working for them. That was two years ago. Ponce called and the rest, as they say, is history.

Constantly hounding Terry, Jason wanted him to either get his brother from another mother Pepper, to join, or hire a third hand so they could get the better gigs. Hesitant to take that kind of responsibility for other people's lives, Terry would say, "It's bad enough I have to put myself between a bullet and my client. It doubles the responsibility when you and I are together, but to add a third person...I don't know if I want that kind of load." So, Ponce became the third hand.

Terry knew Pepper would join them as soon as he got out of the Navy; it was all he talked about. The "brothers" had it all planned out. Pepper would join the service and get as much info out of it as possible while Terry would go into the private sector and learn everything he could. Even if it meant working for free, he would make that sacrifice so they could start their own company and do it their own way.

Pepper and Rowdy had been friends since they were children; growing on the same block the two were inseparable. When they were still in their teens the two formed plan to open their own business, it was a coin toss that decided who would join the military and who would go private. Pepper joined the Navy and Rowdy worked for anyone that he thought he could learn from.

While attending a private academy that trained bodyguards, Terry and Jason met. By the end of the six-week period, they were inseparable. It was during this time they would form a partnership that would last forever. Three years later they hired Ponce, a Puerto-Rican American with a quick wit and skill for business they both admired. Within eight months, they made Ponce a partner and their business doubled.

Completing his last step from the plane, Ponce led the POTC toward a makeshift table, made from a broken piece of plywood crossed over two fifty-five gallon drums. Hearing the sound of an approaching car in the distance did not go undetected by Jason, "looks like Raphael at the wheel," he announced.

"Look alive people, this is not a drill!" Terry warned.

Slowing in front of the bay doors, a black Lincoln Limousine pulled along side of and stopped next to the hangar. Quickly getting out of the vehicle, the driver hurriedly moved to the back door of the sleek car, opening it. A young man of about thirty-five wearing a straw hat exited the rear of the car and swiftly moved inside the building, with the driver hot on his heels.

As both men entered the hangar, they were greeted by the stifling heat. "Bienvidoes, mi amigos, welcome to Colombia!" The hatted man said with a smile, as he embraced the POTC.

"Gracias Señor Stamos, Cuomo estas?" replied the POTC with a laugh. "I am impressed gringo, your Spanish is getting better."

The driver of the limo smiled at Terry and Jason, joining them as his boss and theirs had important things to discuss. "How have you been Raphy?" Jason inquired.

"Man, things are pretty tense about this buyout. The people who live near the plant are pissed that your boss is selling out to Stamos."

Terry cocked his head and asked, "Why would they care?"

"Because this fucker's only interested in the equipment and stocks. Once he sells them, he plans to close the plant. Three thousand people are gonna be out of work."

Jason let out a low whistle and shook his head, "Shit Ter, I hope this goes smooth so we can get out of here in one piece."

"Relax, this trip ain't nothin' but a thang," Terry said, in his best street slang. "Besides, I have dinner reservations waitin' for us and I don't plan on bein' late." All three laughed.

Their revelry was short-lived and broken by all hell breaking loose, as Raphy crossed in front of the half-open hangar doors. Hit mid-chest by several high-powered rounds, most of the contents of large mans chest sprayed onto the dirt floor. Banking away from the open doors, Jason and Terry rolled behind a couple of empty drums and came up with guns blazing. Grabbing the POTC, Ponce dragged him up the stairs to the plane, with Señor Stamos directly behind them.

"Get your ass on the plane!" Terry yelled to Jason, over the noise of the turbines picking up momentum.

"I'm not leaving you here!" Jason shouted back.

"Fuck you, if you think I'm staying, I'll be right behind you!" As Terry shouted those words, the metal wall he was seeking refuge behind suddenly opened up from the spray of automatic machine gun fire. Terry felt a sharp, stinging pain against his left eyebrow, then the warmth of blood running freely down his face. The turbines were at full ready and Ponce yelled at both men to get on the plane.

Another burst over Terry's head had him scrambling for the steps to the plane. Looking over his shoulder, he watched in horror as Jason was practically cut in half by enemy fire. "NOOOOOO!" he screamed.

Ponce was already down the stairs, yanking Terry into the plane. "We can't leave him God dammit!" Terry cried, attempting to pull away from Ponce.

"We don't have a choice Terry, the POTC wanted us to leave you and you're not dead yet!" argued Ponce, as he threw Terry into his seat.

Pressing his face against the oval window of the plane, Terry could no longer see his friend. With fists against the wall, Terry made a decision. Standing up from his seat, he attempted to move to the front of the plane. Blocking his way, Ponce stood in front of him. "We need to get that bleeding under control and that cut sewn up," said Ponce tersely.

"Get out of my way," ordered Terry. The look of death in his eyes was intimidating, even to Ponce. Nodding his head, Ponce stepped aside. Terry made his way forward to the POTC and Señor Stamos. Leaning in close, he stuck his Smith & Wesson .40 caliber handgun in the POTC's face and pulled the trigger. The front of the POTC's pants developed a dark, wet mark, and then he passed out.

Stamos belly laughed and slapped Terry on the back, "Señor has the balls of steel, no?" Smiling, Terry went back to his seat.

"What happened?" asked Ponce frantically.

"No more bullets I guess," Terry mumbled, as he fell into his seat.

Ponce grabbed the gun from his hand and racked the slide, ejecting a live round into the air. Losing his grip on reality, Terry began to laugh. Ponce dropped the round back into the gun, dropped the slide and aimed it at a bulletproof vest draped over a seat. The sound of the unmuffled .40 caliber handgun on the plane was deafening. Ponce's normally bronze skin, turned pale, as the color drained from his face. Terry kept laughing and the POTC who was just coming to from his fainting spell, wet himself again, just to pass out once more. Señor Stamos sat in his seat openmouthed.

Sitting behind the wheel of his eighty-three Blazer four-by, Terry watched Ponce walk over to and hop inside the passenger seat. "I can't believe he's gone," Terry said, his voice barely a whisper.

Ponce handed Terry two thick, number ten, plain white envelopes. Pulling his Spyderco knife from his back pocket, Terry slit them both open. Thumbing through the wad of money, satisfied the agreed upon amount was there, he checked the second envelope, coming to the same conclusion. Waiting patiently and silently for him to finish, Ponce handed him another envelope.

This one was brown and bore the logo S.I. Ltd., Stamos Industries. Terry slit it open and spilled the contents out onto the console between him and Ponce. Handing a handful to Ponce and scooping up the rest for to himself, he began to count.

"Thirteen thousand, two hundred and sixty-four bucks. Fuck me runnin.'" Terry said with disbelief.

"I got eleven thousand, seven hundred and thirty-six right here. Jeezus Ter, that's twenty-five grand above and beyond the fifty large we got for the job!" Countered Ponce.

"Put it back in the envelope, it belongs to Amanda," said Terry quietly. Ponce never said a word. Stuffing the money into the envelope, he returned it to his friend. The two rode back to the office in silence. Ponce waved at Terry as he drove off, with no thoughts of envy for him at that moment. Knowing the job of telling Amanda and the kids that Jason didn't make it, wouldn't be an easy one. Shaking his head sadly, Ponce got into his car and drove home.

Amanda heard Terry pull into the driveway. Coming around the corner of the red tile walkway, leading from the door of their modest three-bedroom home in Lake Elsinore to the driveway, she waved.

"Hey Terry!"

She was in a good mood. Amanda was always in a good mood,

that was one constant in Terry's life. Calling the house to talk with Jason, she would always answer the phone with a melodious tone in her voice. Terry was about to see another side to Amanda.

"Where's Jason, getting the gear out of the truck?" Putting his arms on hers, Terry began to back her up the walk. Standing on her tiptoes, Amanda tried to see if Jason was hiding behind Terry in an attempt to sneak up on her and yell boo. Jason loved to play this game from time to time.

"Amanda..." Her face became stoic, as she looked directly into Terry's eyes, then he saw the pain.

"Oh my God..." she whispered, shaking her head. Pulling her to him, Terry tried to comfort her. Jumping back, Amanda landed a fist across his jaw catching him off guard.

"You bastard! You promised! For Christ sake Terry, you promised me!" Wailing mournfully, Amanda continued to remind Terry of a promise made--the promise of Jason's safe return. Dragging her into the house, Amanda suddenly became dead weight. Scooping her up, Terry carried Amanda into the living room, depositing her on the couch. She fell asleep sobbing in his arms, he was thankful her kids were at their grandmother's. Terry finally gave in to exhaustion and even in sleep, he held her.

Terry awoke with Amanda sitting on his morning erection, by the time Terry realized it was not a dream he was having it was too late, he released deep inside Amanda. She looked down at him, her bangs framing her face, she smiled timidly and thanked him for "being there, I just needed to feel closer to Jason" she lied through her tears as she rolled off and headed to the bathroom in one smooth maneuver.

Terry heard the door lock from the bed, he sat up and couldn't believe what just happened, he grabbed his clothes and turned on the shower in the guest bath down the hall.

Having a Lady MacBeth moment in the shower Rowdy couldn't

scrub hard enough, the best place to cry is in the shower, get it out now and you can be stoic in front of the girl he kept repeating in his head. FUCK, FUCK, FUCK, FUCK.

The day brought the harsh task of packing up the house. "I have something for you," mumbled Terry, as he reached into his coat pocket. Pulling the brown envelope from inside, he handed it to her and having a hard time making eye contact.

"How much is here?" she asked, appearing stunned.

Lying, Terry said, "Forty K, it was his take from the gig, now its yours."

"Terrence Alan Calhoun, since when do you take me for a fool?"

Looking at the ceiling, then to the floor, he asked, "Huh?"

"You guys never clear this kind of money on a gig, never!"

Swallowing hard, trying not to let it show, he answered, "We got a bonus." This time he wasn't lying.

"How much?" she asked, while eyeing him like an Eagle watching a rabbit.

"Twenty-five grand."

"Terry I cant take this much..."

He cut her off. "You don't worry about it. You've got forty large there and another twenty-five in the bank, Ponce transferred the funds this morning. Add to that another three million you've got comin' from the insurance money and if that isn't enough, you also have a twenty-five percent stake in the company. We will keep depositing the earnings every month into this account." Running a thumb over the well-worn account book, he handed it to her.

Amanda sat down at the kitchen table putting her head in her hands, "What else don't I know about my husband's affairs?" she whispered.

"You now know everything," Terry answered.

Standing up, Amanda crossed the cool tile of the kitchen floor, then threw out her arms and hugged Terry's large frame. Hugging her back, but before he could pull away, she kissed him full on the mouth. He actually enjoyed it for a brief second, and then pushed Amanda back.

"Sorry," Terry whispered.

Moving toward the door, with a shaking voice, Terry said, "Call me when you get settled, or if you need anything."

He left two large and very long black stripes down the street as he left, fuck me runnin,' he said to himself, as he gripped the steering wheel.

Jason was gone. Terry had broken his promise. As he drove away, Terry knew he would never go back to the business again. He would sell out his share, make sure Amanda and the kids were set, but he would never go back.

Never say never.... and never say you wont go back.

FMR

CHAPTER 2
MEXICO 1993

It's truly amazing what the human mind can hone in on when one is in the midst of a major adrenaline rush. Gunfire's blasting all around and you have some asshole checking out the local beauties, as you're flying through some shit hole of a town at one hundred miles per hour.

"Wow Rowdy, didja' see that one! The one in red?" asked Ponce. He was in love again, with only a glimpse to go by.

Now you wouldn't think that the mind could actually perceive such a vision of loveliness with the speeds we were traveling, would you? Well, there are some things that just stand out, especially when you're in the middle of nowhere. The place just had death for its color--browns and grays were pretty much it, except for her. Standing tightly pressed against the wall of some worn out building, she tried desperately to stay out of our way.

Her long, black hair and red dress were such a contrast to her surroundings; you couldn't help but notice her. Her dress could barely contain her tits, so I imagine Ponce couldn't help but notice her either. He will forever be a breast man. I, on the other hand, was distracted, but not by tits and ass.

"God dammit Terry, I'm talkin' to you!" he shouted again, attempting to get my attention. And in case ya'll haven't figured it out yet, Rowdy and Terry are one in the same...me. But, we'll get to the nickname later.

I felt a stinging slap against my cheek and jaw line. "What the fuck?" I asked, rubbing my cheek. "Whatcha' do that for?"

"Feel like joinin' the rest of us kiddies for all this fun!?" Ponce asked with sarcasm, while reloading his AK 47.

"Sorry man, I was just thinkin' about Jason. You know that son-of-a-bitch Allbright, said this was supposed to be a walk in the park?"

"I truly believe he was bullshittin' ya dude!"

I shook my head in disgust as I glanced over at Ponce. There he was, in a fit of laughter, while I was trying to figure out what way in particular I'd like to painfully separate Allbright from his balls. "Gee, ya think?" I asked.

"Well, if we live through this, remind me to kill him!"

"Yeah, if and when brother-man, if and when!"

With the slap throwing me back into the game, as team leader I had to quickly assess the situation: we had Pepper, M.C. and Tim in the lead car. Ponce, Mr. Yakamoto (the POTC) and myself in a fast second. Tom, Alex and Axel as cover in third, with Senior, Roger and Todd, holding strong on the rear. Our convoy had just sped through some toilet of a town even God must have forgotten. The team, still showing its approval or disapproval of the woman in red, also had a heated debate going as to how pretty the girls were south of the border. To top it all off, we had some very bad Mexicans shooting very big guns and we were their target.

To add the proverbial fly to the ointment, Pepper was trying to drive and eat a hamburger at the same time. Actually, that wasn't the irritating part. He executed fine driving style as far as I could see, as he maneuvered his vehicle to avoid running over chickens and pigs. As Pepper swerved to miss a small animal of some kind, M.C. attempted to tuck in a dip. Because of the constant careening of the car, he kept spilling his precious chew and that pissed him off to no end. Unfortunately for the rest of us, we got to hear just how pissed off he was. Our voice activated, team radios were so sensitive, that if one farted, the rest of us heard it. "How can you eat a hamburger at a time like this!?" demanded M.C.

"The thang about it is..." You could barely understand a damn thing that came out of Pepper's overly stuffed mouth. "I got this thang long 'afore them SOB's started chasin' us! If you think I'm gonna just throw it out the window cause a few guns are goin' off, you're outta your shit for brains mind! It took me two days to find somebody that could even make me a hamburger!"

"Two days!? What the fuck have you been asking for? It's just a hamburger for Chrissake!"

Shoveling in another mouthful, Pepper continued, "Everyone just kinda looked at me funny when I asked for a burger, so I just kept lookin!"
"You stupid, southern son-of-a-bitch! If you would speak English correctly, you might get what you asked for. Friggin' moron," M.C. mumbled.

"So, whatcha' trying to say?" I looked over at Ponce and all he did was shrug, as if to say, "Hey, he's your brother!"

I looked behind us and could see that Tom appeared to be struggling with the steering of his Ford Taurus. "Tom, you okay back there?" I asked

"Musta taken a hit to the pump!" he answered, as Axel leaned far out the window to return fire from the truck behind them. Tom kept yelling at him to get down, but it was too late, the Mexicans took care of him. Taking a direct hit to the head and spraying gray matter everywhere, Axel tumbled out of the car. To add insult to injury, Senior flattened him out while trying to tighten the distance between him and his teammates. If you knew Axel, you'd realize that was no easy feat. "Christ I never could stand him, mumbled Tom.

Senior jumped in with, "Hey Tom! This car was not designed to run over such big fuckin' objects! Oh by the way, I heard that! No one would believe you liked him anyway, not even a little bit!" Senior was laughing his ass off, as he resumed his own personal gun battle.

We caught some reference from Tom about Senior's mother, when next we heard what sounded like a grunt of pain.

I needed to get a handle on the predicament, 'cause things were not good. "SitRep!" I ordered to all. It was time to pull something out of our asses...and fast.

Senior was first to report, "Roger's been hit pretty bad and our ammo's running low!"

"I'm OK," shouted Roger, "it went clean through!"

Tom piped in with his two bits, "I have ammo, my car is making a funny noise and I want to go home now!"

"Hey you guys," said M.C. softly, "I have an idea."

"But I haven't finished my burger yet!" whined Pepper.

"Take it easy, it'll all be over in a minute," he replied. Whenever M.C. got this certain quiet voice, you knew there would be a very loud noise behind it. "Here, take this for a sec, OK?"

"Oh Jeeeeeezus! Give me a warnin' the next time ya want me ta hold a grenade!" shouted Pepper.

M.C. positioned himself to throw the grenade, then looked to Pepper and shouted, "OK! Give it up!" Pepper pulled the pin and handed M.C. his burger. During the confusion, he stuffed the grenade in his mouth, as M.C. threw out the hamburger. A direct hit to the windshield of the bad guy, started M.C. laughing when he saw the look on the drivers face.

"Hahahahaha, fuckin' A!" he shouted, "Did you see that guy?"

Just as I was about to warn Pepper about the live grenade, he spat it out the window. I'd never seen anything like it! The fuckin' thing hit the ground, bounced right over the roof of our car, rolled under Tom's car, then exploded against the bad guys truck! Seemed like Mr. Murphy, (the unseen guest at every OP), caught a ride with the Mexicans. Thankfully for us, the Gods of war were behind us that day.

I saw Pepper look back at the exploding vehicle, "Gawdamn! Do you have any idea what it's gonna take for me to replace that burger!?"

M.C. laughed, and full of satisfaction answered, "Two days, I know!" To the rest of us he said, "OK everyone, let's go home!"

Pepper continued to give M.C. an ear-full over his lost burger, Gawdammit' about this, that and another. The one thing you have to understand is that Pepper loves hamburgers. He could eat them for every meal.

"Uh, Rowdy? Listen, we have one small problem," said M.C.

"What the hell is it now M.C.?"

In his best Pepper impersonation he said, "The thang about it is...I just looked into the rear view mirror and there's still one more truck back there, with lots more bad guys. Oh yeah, these guns are fully automatic! Uh, I guess that would be two small problems!"

Looking behind us and seeing the truck moving fast on Tom, I ordered, "Deal with it!" I'd just about reached the end of my rope on this gig. I looked over at Ponce. "Ya know? It really pisses me off that he can be so calm at a time like this!"

Ponce, ever the quipster, laughed, "Just you wait till he runs out of Copenhagen!"

Well, fuck me! I couldn't remember the last time a simple bodyguard gig had been run so ass backwards. What the hell did we get ourselves into? I was asking myself. I began to think back. Back to before this Op was dropped on us...back to before I signed over my soul...

CHAPTER 3
SOUTHERN CALIFORNIA
"TWO MONTHS EARLIER"

Okay, so I'm a son-of-a-bitch, I'd be the first to admit that one. Ask anyone who knows me. Christ, better yet, ask my wife. I'm sure she could come up with a few choice words to describe me. In fact, son-of-a-bitch might even be one of the nicer ones.

Slamming the door to my home didn't relieve any of the raging testosterone surging through my body, but I think I made my point. At least she knew I was pissed. She, being Janet Calhoun, my wife. Talk was no longer an easy thing for us. Between the arguments and hurtful words, an uncomfortable silence formed between us. There were some days that I swear to God, I should have listened to my brother.

"The thang about it is...," Pepper would say, "bed her or live with her, just don't marry her."

"Shit!" I said out loud, as I slammed the door to my pickup and saw Janet headed straight for me. As she came closer to my Dodge, I could see her tear stained cheeks. All right, so I felt a momentary stab of guilt, but believe me, it wouldn't last long. I couldn't afford the emotions she wanted to see from me.

After seeing what human beings can do to one another, you have to learn to shut down. To turn off that part of you that grieves for the mother who lost her son to a drive by shooter or the rage of a fellow officer killed in the line of duty. The problem for me? I didn't know how to turn that switch back on anymore or worse, I didn't know if I really wanted to. It was easier to deal with everything in my life with the cold efficiency I had learned from my line of work. No emotion, no depth, no pain. Yeah...right.

"Look Terry," began Janet, "I'm still pissed, OK? There's just no way in hell I'm going to let you go to work, without telling you I love you."

"Janet, ya know I do too."

I hoped I could come off appearing to be less than the ogre she believed me to be. With a callused finger, I reached to wipe away her tears.

"But I've got to go to work."

"Go then! You're very good at leaving!"

"Come on Janet, don't be like this."

As if searching for something, she looked into my eyes--for what, only she knew. With a quivering chin, she turned and ran back into our home. "Fuck!" I said out loud. So much for trying to be Mr. Nice Guy. Revving up my pickup, punching it into reverse and with a quick squeal of the tires and faint smell of rubber, I headed out for my hour-long drive to work. An hour can be a fleeting moment for some men in reflection. For a man such as myself, an hour may as well be eternity, with too many demons to wrestle and too many nameless faces.

More often than not, I would use this time to reflect on my life. Now there's a real party. Of course you could ask, which one. I led a regular life and a not so regular life. In my regular life, I paid taxes, had the wife and kids and held an honorable job as a Peace Officer. The other life, that of a bodyguard, held unique perils of its own that only a select few outside of the industry could understand. These two opposing facets of my life headed for a collision course and there wasn't a Goddamn thing I could do about it.

Janet was aware of my life as Peace Officer and vaguely aware of my bodyguard gigs. I kept most of this part of my life a secret from her. She knew I was in the protect biz, but I could be in some shit hole, piss poor country and Janet wouldn't have a clue as to where I was. A bag always sat at the ready, filled with the basics of what I would need for my next assignment.

"Son-of-a-bitch," I thought to myself, she knew my life and how I lived it before we married. Why do women always try to change you? The worst part? I really needed those assignments. If I weren't hopping on a plane for God knows where, within about three months or so, I'd start to feel like a trapped animal looking to bite off its leg to be free. They helped me to maintain at least some semblance of sanity in my life. The down times I had while waiting for the next gig, were the periods our marriage suffered from the most and we fought often. Between my edginess and Janet's tears, we both said things we regretted and wished we could take back. Words said in anger are like a pierce into the heart, they can never be taken back.

I loved the adrenaline rush that went with the job. There's something to be said for a job well done, that you also enjoy. To know you are a part of something important, exciting and yes, extremely dangerous. So many things could go wrong on an Op and so much training and preparation went into them. I was good at my work and excelled at it. It seemed to be the only true constant in my sorry-ass excuse for a life. Jesus Christ, I ought a be locked up in a rubber room somewhere and the fuckin' key thrown away, I thought in disgust.

I don't know about ya'll, but I hate fights before going to work. Our argument du jour was different from most. Janet found out about my involvement in a short-lived affair. Despite the initial fiery accusations, I continued to deny everything. She didn't buy it and beat me down until I had no choice but to confess. My indiscretion had finally caught up with me.

"It doesn't mean I don't love you Janet!" I shouted. So loudly in fact, I thought the plaster might start to crack and fall on top of us. "God dammit, what am I supposed to do? You pull away from me every time I try to touch you!"

"Screw you and your warped sense of honor! How could you do this to me? You and your Knights of the Round Table go off saving the world, but when I need you, you find some excuse to run away and go do something or somebody!"

Thankfully, I was about ready to head out the door, because I hated to see a woman cry and cry she did. "I can't deal with this shit right now Janet, I just can't."

Shaken out of my thoughts by a blaring horn, told me my light had changed green. Hitting the accelerator, I immediately chastised myself for being less than aware of my surroundings. That kinda shit will get ya killed, I told myself through gritted teeth. I shoved my favorite Clint Black CD into the player and cranked up the volume, forcing my thoughts into the background.

Pleased to finally reach the parking lot to the police station, I knew I could put my memories of the day behind me and focus on something else. Even if a few hours of relief were all I'd have, it would be better than nothing. Dealing with a gang-banger at that moment had more appeal than dealing with my wife.

CHAPTER 4
THE ZOO

With the evening briefing concluded, and our assignments given, it was time for me to go The Zoo. Affectionately named by the men and women who worked this sector, The Zoo deserved its nickname. Within those two square miles of Section 8 housing, all forms of the human animal lived there, and we were its keepers. Inside the invisible cages of this place, we had: single mothers struggling to make a living for their fatherless children, as well as whole families who were attempting to overcome their misfortunes to gain a better life for themselves. Whores, pimps, crack heads and gang members were the predators of our little corner of the world.

Before dealing with the animals, I'd make a little stop in Safe Haven. Granted, The Haven may not have been the kind of place someone used to Beverly Hills might drive through-but I felt it was my last gasp of semi clean air before entering my sector. Okay, it wasn't much to look at, with buildings artistically smattered with graffiti, and winos pissing on the walls. Nonetheless, I would take The Haven over The Zoo any day. The other reason I looked forward to The Haven, was to meet with a unique individual and friend. One who had earned my respect, love and undying trust.

Wallace G. Bennett, Chief Gunners Mate, Navy retired. An aging man with balding head, slower reflexes and a paunch that he always patted proudly. Pepper had served under him, and introduced us. Respect given by a man like the Chief can be a hard fought thing. Equally difficult, is a man who earns mine.

Chief worked as a rent-a-cop, providing security for a small sector of his own. Truth be known, the job made him feel useful. Money was nothing he had much use for and he had plenty of it for his needs. "Rowdy," he would say, "it's like a good fuck. If you don't use your dick once in a while, what good is it?"

I pulled into the gas station Chief watched over at that time of night. Smiling, I watched as he waved a muscled, tattooed arm in greeting. I parked, then quickly got out of my Crown Victoria cruiser. Meeting me outside the door, he offered his thick hand for me to shake. As usual, he hit me with a roaring salutation. "So meat whistle, how the hell are ya?"

Chuckling, I answered, "Well, you know, same shit different day."

With a slap on my back, Chief laughed, "Come on Terry, time to get this shit out of my car and into yours." Separating, we moved to the rear of our vehicles. After opening the trunks, Chief began to hand me bags of weaponry that could, quite frankly, be used against a small country, if I were in the mood to declare war on it. I believed in being prepared and The Zoo was no exception. Armed to the teeth were these animals, and yes, they did bite. My favorite saying for this district, "That which doesn't kill me, better run away pretty fuckin' fast."

When Chief first learned about the territory I was to cover, he took me aside and said, "Son, I know you think you're Superman, but a bullet from some of those toys will go through you like a stone through a pile of shit. You're gonna need more than your standard issue Glock 45 and that pussy of a stick you call an Asp. I'm serious here boy, ya can't let Janet become a widow because you were outgunned."

Well, I did have my own private stash, and realized that Chief was right. The bulletproof vests the department handed out weren't enough against some of the shit one could find themselves against in The Zoo. So, I got myself some extra backup. (Just for those little emergencies that could sometimes arise. And they always do)

Once gathered, I asked Chief if he would hold my stash for me, bringing it to The Haven whenever our shifts ran together. I couldn't very well have the department seeing my toys, now could I?

"Sure son, whatcha got in there anyway?" He asked, eyeing my goody bags.

As if reading a weapon's report, I stood at attention, took a deep breath and listed everything I had. "Sir! I have a H&K MP5 suppressed with laser sight and six spare magazines, Glock 18 fully automatic machine pistol with four spare mags, two Def-Tec flash bang grenades, two Oleoresin Capsicum (pepper spray) grenades and a load bearin' tactical vest with a Balaclava black hood, Sir!" I continued to stand at attention until the Chief's laughter forced me into a parade rest.

Every night we worked the same shift; the Chief brought my precious cargo. If by chance the Chief had the night off, I'd run by his place to pick it up myself. Claire, his wife, took to me right away, considering me a member of their family. She would always pack an extra sandwich for me inside of her husband's lunch box. I remember hoping Janet and I could reach that many years of marriage.

After my backup was neatly hidden away in my trunk, Chief and I would just kick back against our cars, shootin' the shit. We seemed to fill a void that existed in the other. For Chief, he could revel in his glory days, and impart a bit of his hard learned wisdom onto to me. For myself, I learned a great deal from the old man. An understanding ear is what I found in him, that I could use from time to time, when there was no one else to hear the bullshit. For Pepper and myself, he was the father we never had.

"So, how's that mud suckin,' worthless puddle of goat piss step brother of yours?" You could always count on Chief for a way with words.

"He's just fine Chief."

Taking a long draw off his cigarette, he just looked at me for a long minute. I knew what was coming next, as he put out his cigarette under his shoe. "Out with it boy. I know something is gnawin' on ya."

Lighting a Marlboro, I shook my head in disbelief at his ability to see inside of me. Just looking me over, he knew what kind of mood I was in. That day, I was in a real shitter. I slowly exhaled trying to think of some smart-ass thing to say. However, I could see in his eyes that I would really be in for a ration of shit if I tried to BS him. Chief always knew when I had something in my craw. "Janet and I had another fight." I answered simply. "I mean a real ball breaker."

"Son, believe me, being married forty-two years has given me my share of battles. We always make up. Claire, God love her, always manages to find the good inside of this old warhorse. Tell a woman what she wants to hear boy. Make sure she knows you love her. Show her, don't just tell her."

I always appreciated anything that Chief could offer in the ways of the world. "Hey Chief? You ever cheat on Claire?"

"Lots of times," came back the answer, with a devilish grin. "I was young and stupid like you are."

"Does she know?"

"Of course she does Terry."

"So...what happened?"

"Let me tell you something son. I never rubbed her nose in any of it and I never did it in this country."

"So that crap they teach at the academy, 'bout the 50 miles from the flagpole. That's not horse shit?"

"Terry, listen to the old Chief, you need to get your priorities straight. You don't get anywhere in life by playin' stupid." Lighting another non-filter Camel, he drew deeply from it. For a few minutes, we stayed in our own thoughts. He, I suppose, thinking back to his youth, and I was thinking about my fight with Janet.

Taking one more drag from my Marlboro, I crushed it with my

shoe, exhaling loudly. "I guess you're right Chief, I'm the stupid one."

"Yes, you are, but I love you anyway. Even now, Janet's ready to throw your worthless, no good, piece of monkey nuts, low life ass out of the house!"

"Thanks Chief, now I know I'm truly loved."

"Get to work God dammit! I'll see you at dinner!"

Throwing the Chief a smart salute, I jumped into my cruiser. I liked knowing he was near my back door. There had been more than a few occasions where the Chief had kept an animal from escaping the zoo. The personnel within the police department admired and respected him for his courage and sense of duty to the community.

All I knew was that I loved the crusty old bastsrd.

CHAPTER 5
FAIR WINDS AND FOLLOWING SEAS

Putting on my business face, I got ready to deal with the animals. I knew instantly when I entered my beat sector. To me, it was as if the earth's life simply got sucked away by the animal life that dwelled there. There were no trees, no grass, and no flowers. Dead, everything was dead.

I couldn't help recalling the constant efforts made by outside communities to help in this less fortunate one. Used hypodermic needles, spent condoms and empty shells from illegal guns were what these caring individuals got for their efforts. The good, law-abiding folks who lived in this hell were too afraid to speak against those who ran The Zoo with an iron fist and an AK assault rifle. That shit hole was really too far-gone to do anything for it anyway.

From what my XO had to say at the briefing, I figured The Zoo would be the place for Johnny The Torch to hit. Word on the street was that a major arson deal was going down, and his name came up. The perfect insurance scam. Flame the dilapidated ruins of the warehouse and projects district, and make way for new development.

Stopping my cruiser, I shut down all the lights. I allowed myself a moment for my eyes to adjust to the total darkness. As they did, I caught a movement from the corner of my eye. I saw a shadow disengage itself from a building about twenty-five yards away. "Come to Papa." I said to myself, as I leaned toward the windshield. Peering into the darkness, I saw the shadow headed straight for me. The prey began to move unsuspectingly down the alley toward the hunter.

Suddenly, the silence broke with a piercing, "Beep...beep...beep." "Shit!" I said aloud between gritted teeth as I began to wrestle the pager inside the car, trying desperately to find a way to shut off the fuckin' thing. The Torch stood frozen, staring down the alley, searching the darkness. Jumping as if he got shot in the ass, Torch took off to the opposite end of the alley.

"Shit..Fuck...God dammit!!" I shouted as I hit the switch that turned on the red and blue rotators. Starting the car, I slammed my foot onto the accelerator.

My patrol car lurched up the alley with Torch at full gallop and about to reach the end of it. A few more yards, I'd be home free. That son-of-a-bitch was really starting to piss me off. The charging car continued to pick up speed and I was gaining on him.

While trying to turn off my piece of shit pager, my patrol car began careening side to side taking out dumpsters and ruining the paint job on yet another vehicle. Finally finding the switch, I ended its incessant beeping.

"Jeeeeeezus!" I shouted as I looked up to see Torch hitting the street, making a hard right onto the sidewalk. Realizing I was moving too fast for this turn, I prepared for the right-hander that was quickly approaching. Hitting the brakes, sawing the steering wheel, then kicking the gas pedal to the floor, I closed the distance between us. The Torch was tiring fast. I cranked the wheel of my car and veered toward the sidewalk right in front of him. The Torch hit the car at near full speed and flew over the hood landing face down on the pavement.

Snatching the little black box that instigated these events, I pushed the light display and saw three words waiting for me, "Call Allbright ASAP." I didn't know it then, but these words were going to change my life forever. "Shit Richard, this better be important." Glancing out the window, I shook my head at the Torch, who was sprawled out tasting cement.

With holstered Glock 45 and collapsed ASP, I slowly removed myself from my vehicle and took a long stretch. Again, I shook my head at the weasel dick, as he lay on the sidewalk. Taking my time, I meandered toward him, enjoying every minute of it. I folded my arms across my fifty-two inch chest and lightly tapped at the Torch with a dress polished shoe. While standing at 6'3," I looked down on the pathetic animal and couldn't help but laugh, "damn Johnny,

25

we gotta stop meeting like this. What are people gonna say?"

"Fuck you, man! I didn't do a God damn thing!"

Squatting down to his level, I could feel my thighs threatening to burst through the fabric of my trousers. I wanted to look the little piss worm right in the eyes. "So, whatcha runnin' for if you're such a fine upstandin' individual?"

"I got nothing to say to you, Pig!" he shouted.

Reaching out with my heavy hand, I lifted the Torch off the ground by his oily hair. With bloodied hands, he started to reach behind him, pawing at my fist so that I might lose my grip. Therefore, I found it my duty to jab the piece of maggot excrement in the solar plexus, forcing him to drop his arms instantly, fighting for breath.

"Look ya little prick, I don't wanna be gettin' any diseases from ya, so keep your fuckin' hands on the car." With that, I threw him against the hood of my cruiser. "You know the drill asshole, spread 'em!" Leaning in close, although the his stench told me I shouldn't, I asked, "Ya don't have anything that could hurt me do ya?" Turning his face toward me, Torch spit at me.

With a weighty forearm, I brought it down on Torch's shoulder with such speed, that he didn't have time to react. I could hear the clean snap as I made the connection to his bone and flesh. "That was assault on a police officer!" I growled, as I grabbed him by the arms, and with a twisting motion, deftly brought them behind his back.

"AAAAAAHHHH!! Jesus Christ, you broke my fuckin' arm!"

"Actually, I broke your collar bone. The more you move, the more this will hurt."

"Fuck you man!"

As I completed my search, I felt a lump around Johnny's ankle.

"Hmmmm......I wonder what this is? Certainly can't be your dick."

"Shit." The resignation in his voice told me that he knew he was going to be busted for possession of a firearm.

"Hey Torch, since when did they start allowing convicted felons to carry a concealed weapon?" Putting the vermin's gun into my back pocket, I then grabbed him by the T-shirt with a fisted paw. His slight body was dangling inches from the pavement. "Who hired you for this job?"

The guttural groans that escaped Torch's lips, hinted to me that he was near suffocation. Loosening my hold slightly, I set Torch back on his feet. He quickly gasped for a breath, pulling in the warm humid air.

The jerk off was yankin' my chain, so in my most firm, I'm not takin' any more of your bullshit voice, I said, "I'm only going to ask this one more time."

"Okay! Okay!" He squealed. "Jesus fuckin' Christ, it ain't worth dyin' over! Calhoun, take me to jail. The guy who comes to get me out is...uhhhhhh." I could hear the moan that whispered out of his chalky lips and his body slammed into mine. Looking into Torch's eyes, I saw that they were empty. I had seen that look many times before and knew it very well.

Suddenly, the windshield of my patrol car shattered. "What the fuck!?" I said out loud. Someone was using me and my car for target practice. I could hear the distant sound of tires squealing as the shooter made his escape. Glancing at the dead man, I felt a seconds worth of sympathy for the wretched animal as I reached for my lapel mike.

Drawing my attention away from Torch, were several people assembled to find out what the disturbance was about. I heard someone shout, "Hey, this guy's shot too!"

Wondering how that could be, I knew there was no one else in

27

the area. As I approached the near lifeless body, grief seized me. "Chief!" My mind screamed and I felt that my heart had been ripped out, as I watched the hand that took it. Unknown to me, Chief had seen a suspicious vehicle enter The Zoo. Thinking only of covering my ass, he investigated it. He never heard the fatal shot of the silenced bullet. Dropping to the ground, I cradled my friend, encircling my arms around him. With a handkerchief, I gently wiped away the blood from his mouth. "Everything will be Okay. Hold on Chief...please."

As I reached for my mike, the old sailor wheezed, "Did we get him boy?" My eyes began to fill and overflow, the heated tears running down my face. The Chief began to cough up blood as he gasped for his last precious breath.

"Yeah Chief, we got him." I answered, clawing for the lapel mike.

Chief reached for my hand as his own shook from the death grip that was upon him. "Son, tell Claire...she was...the only love..." With a gurgle and sigh, Chief died.

With a tight controlled voice, I made the call. "One-Paul-Five, I have two men down! Expedite emergency services and back-up!" A moment of silence brought back a subdued voice.

Holding my friend tightly in my arms, I rocked him gently. The usual animal activities began around me, as more people came outside to see what had happened. I was unaware of most of it. I vaguely heard the sound of wailing sirens in the distance. Closing my eyes, I whispered, "Good-bye my friend, may the wind guide your sails."

CHAPTER 6
DEEP BREATHS

Watching Chief's body bag being zipped up and hoisted into the ambulance was one of the most difficult things I'd ever done. Participating in war twice over, dealing with all that life had to throw at him, then his life force ended in seconds from a bullet never meant for him.

No two ways about it, the night just kept getting worse. Condolences were coming in left and right, and it was all I could do to hold myself together. Chief touched so many, and his presence would be missed by more than just me. Right then, I didn't really care about anyone else but his family, and I needed to get to them. Two things were about to stand in my way, or so I thought.

"Calhoun, I'm Sergeant Davies and this is Sergeant Farrow from Homicide," he said, gesturing to the older man in the wrinkled suit.

"Yeah, I know," I replied uneasily.

"Calhoun," began Davies, "we've already checked with witnesses and have an idea of how things went down tonight, you are free to go for now."

I couldn't believe what I was hearing. Being harassed by these cheap suits was the norm, so I assumed they were setting me up somehow. If I waited long enough, maybe I'd hear, "Smile you're on candid camera!"

Farrow took over, "Sorry to hear about Chief. We know he was a friend of yours, and I felt privileged to have met him. Go on, get out of here."

Standing there looking like a dumb shit, I nodded to the suits and headed for my cruiser. As well known as Chief was, who could have guessed how many lives he had touched.

Sitting heavily in the car, I just closed my eyes. I convinced my commanding officer that I should be the one to tell Claire that her husband was dead. Taking a couple deep breaths and exhaling slowly, I reached for the cell phone to call Pepper. Christ, I knew he was going to take it hard.

Pepper picked up on the line with a gruff, "Whaddaya want?" Knowing my brother better than anyone, I realized I probably intruded on some skin play and a piece of ass.
"Pepper, I need to talk to you. It's important."

"Hold on."

I could hear muffled voices in the background and the slam of a door. Apparently someone was not very happy.

"OKAY, so you ruined my fun in the sin bin, what the hell is so important?"

With much difficulty, I explained all that transpired earlier that evening. "Bro, I need you to pick up Ruth and take her to Claire's." As Chief's daughter, I did not want her to find out from anyone else that her father had met his end. "She needs to be there when Claire's told."

Sensing that Pepper was struggling with his emotions I shouted, "Pepper!" I had to find a way to get him through the pain for just a little while to deal with the situation at hand. With almost a whisper I continued, "I can't do it alone bro, I need your help."

Pepper took a moment to pull himself together, I knew how hard it must have been for him. "I'll take care of it, see ya shortly," he said quietly.

Disconnecting the call, I placed one to Janet. In a businesslike fashion, I relayed to her everything that had happened. I needed to be devoid of emotion as much as possible. It was all I could do to maintain the small amount of composure I had when I heard her soft voice answer. "I'll be home as fast as I can, but I need to be with

Claire right now."

"I understand," she whispered. There was shakiness to Janet's voice that told me she was thinking that this death could have easily been mine. "I'm sorry about the Chief. I really liked him."

She hung up the line and I had one more call left to make. About to retrieve my SAT phone from the back of the car, I changed my mind. "Fuck it Allbright, you can wait."

With that business done, I headed to the station to get my pickup. Careful not to let anyone see me, I stowed my gear away in my truck, and made my way to Claire's house. As I pulled into the driveway, Pepper pulled in with Ruth and her kids. Her eyes were puffy from tears shed, but she managed to get it together for her mother's sake. I helped Pepper with the kids, along with their belongings, and headed into the house. Until 0200 hours in the morning, Pepper and I kept vigil over Claire and Ruth. With the women finally asleep, I asked Pepper if he could go back to my place to stay with Janet.

"I don't want her to wake up and be pissed 'cause I'm not there, but I have to stay here".

Pepper understood what I was trying to tell him and gave me a quick hug. He looked over his shoulder at me again before closing the door behind him. As the door shut, I began to pace, it's my favorite way of being able to think something through. Another habit was to rub at the scar I got from Colombia with Jason. Somehow, it made me feel he was helping me to solve a problem. Starting over at the meeting at the gas station with Chief, I replayed everything out in my head. Everything from the wave hello, to the standing order to vacate the premises to get to work. Repeatedly I ran it in my mind. Repeatedly, I arrived at the same conclusion. There was nothing I could have done to stop what had happened, yet I wasn't satisfied with that answer. I still felt it was my fault for Chief's death. Sitting on the couch, I held my head in my hands. I was so caught up with my own thoughts, that I never heard Ruth who had been standing behind a shelf watching me.

31

She had lost her father, but seemed to feel so much sympathy for me. Hearing my quiet rantings as I acted out what had happened, Ruth knew I felt responsible and tried to let me know I was not to blame. "Terry?" She whispered, as she slowly walked toward me. Sitting next to me on the couch, she rested her arm across my back. "My father took risks that only he was responsible for. No one else can take that from him."

I looked into her tired, red eyes, and again mine began to fill. Together we reached out and held onto each other. Finally getting my shit together, I told Ruth with the funeral two days away, she should get some rest. In agreement, she looked into my eyes again. I wanted so badly to kiss her, but didn't. She whispered, "Goodnight Terry."

Leaning against the couch, I watched as Ruth padded her way down the hallway to the guest room. Alone once more, the little tape in my head rewound itself and started playing again. I went back to the Chief's wave hello and his order to vacate the premises to get to work...

Although a very difficult night, all was quiet in the Bennett household. A light rapping at the door caused me to drag my exhausted ass to it. Checking to see who it was, I was relieved to see Pepper, and let him in.

"Ya know, they got this new invention called sleep, it cures that black bag look under your eyes. Ya outta try it, ya look like shit. Go home Ter, Janet is waitin.'"

Nodding my acknowledgment I asked, "Is she still pissed?"

Pepper walked me to my truck. "Nah, whatever ya'll had goin' on, she's put on the back burner. Just git on home." Putting a concerned hand on my shoulder he told me, "There was nothin' you could have done."

Climbing into the cab of my truck, I felt the weight of so many things on my shoulders. Just wanting to sleep, I headed for home and Janet.

Pulling into the driveway, I saw Janet standing on our porch holding a cup of coffee. Halfway pouring myself out of my truck, I slowly lumbered toward her. Her nervousness was obvious by the way she chewed on her lower lip and I wondered what thing in particular she was dwelling on. Deciding it wasn't the time to worry about it, I just wanted a hug, a shower, and then some shuteye. I was too fuckin' out of it to really do much else.

Janet gave me that quick once over. "Jesus honey, didn't you sleep at all? Come on, let's get you inside."

Taking my hand, she attempted to lead the way. I pulled my hand back and she watched as my tired body walked away. Making my way down the hallway, I began to remove my gear. Janet walked along with me to catch it all. Janet learned early on, that if she didn't want it on the floor, she was gonna have to help me with it. By the time I reached the bathroom, I was nude. Brushing aside the shower curtain, I turned on the cold water. There's something to be said about water so cold it almost hurts. It gives a clarity of mind, and cleansing that I can't get any other way.

"Shit, that's cold!" I said through chattering teeth. Quickly lathering my body and shampooing my trimmed flat top, I stood under the frigid water. Intending to set all the shit aside for a more appropriate time to dwell on it, I bowed my head under the showerhead. Resting my hands against the wall to rinse away the soap and shampoo, I looked down and could see blood mingling with soap before it ran down the drain. I didn't realize that I still had the Chief's blood on me. Fitting I guess, to watch the old man's blood mix with the cold water. Janet tossed me a towel as I brushed the shower curtain open and left a cup of decaf coffee to warm my body.

With nothing more than a towel wrapped around my waist and the hot cup of java, I made my way to the bedroom. Walking to my bed, I set my coffee aside and took a good long stretch. Then, I unholstered my gun from the duty belt, dropped the magazine and racked the slide, ejecting the live bullet into the air. Catching it with my free hand, I shuffled to the closet and to my private, nonofficial stash. Looking at the lone bullet I'd just ejected, made me shake my head, this shit the department makes me carry is about as worthless as tits on a boar hog. I hid it away in one of the many compartments that I keep under lock and key so that none of the kids can accidentally stumble across it.

"Ahhh. Yes," I said, eyeing the custom made, hand loaded bullets nestled in the plus two magazine. Taking my Glock 21, I dropped the slide with an authoritative thwack. Now this, this is the real shit. I ran a finger along the 15, .230 grain Speer hollow points. Most folks in my profession, or maybe I should say professions, referred to these little beauts as "flying ashtrays."

Setting my gun on the nightstand, I lit a cigarette. With another long stretch and draw off the Marl, I decided to check for messages on my E-mail. God, ain't technology grand!

"Don't stay up too late, honey." Janet called out to me.

"Nah, don't worry babe, I'm walkin' wounded right now. Just a few minutes in my mailbox and I'll be right there."

Janet crawled under the sheets and closed her eyes. I knew Chief's death hadn't been easy on her.

Logging on and waiting for the welcome screens to clear, I heard my "hello gorgeous" wav telling me I had some mail. Clicking on the mail icon, I quickly glanced over it all: a note from my mom reminding me I have a grandmother who adores me, (justifiably so, I might add) My ever elusive joke pal had sent a handful of funnies, which I was in no mood for.

Hmmm, one of these days I need to do some diggin' and find out if this is a he or a she, I thought to myself. The rest appeared to be junk mail. As I read each one, I deleted it as I scrolled. Then, I saw one that for some reason, stood out. Looking at it carefully, I decided to open the file. What appeared to be some schpeel on a pyramid scam, was in fact, an encrypted message.

"It's a go for Mexico. You know the training site, be there in one week." This was Allbright's way of confirmation.

My XO approved the leave I'd need to attend the training session Allbright was assembling. He pointedly told me not to make an appearance back to work until I took care of my personal business. He knew how close Chief and I were. I deleted the note from Allbright, finished out my mail, then, dragging ass, finally made my way to bed.

Tossing the towel aside I crawled under the soft, cool, linen sheets. As I stamped out my cigarette, I could hear Janet's even breathing, and knew she was asleep. All I could see was Ruth's face burning into my mind. Closing my eyes, I fell into a deep dreamless sleep.

CHAPTER 7
PREPARATIONS

The day before the funeral was particularly difficult for me. Claire had asked me to take Chief's dress whites to the mortuary. That wasn't even the worst part of the day -- it was yet to come.

Arriving at the mortuary, I asked some peon if I could visit with Chief. All I wanted to do was have a private good-bye with my friend. Shaken after seeing him, it took every ounce of willpower I had to keep from killing someone.

Whoever it was that prepared Chief for the viewing, didn't know him or know of him. This person made him look like Ronald Reagan on his way to a fuckin' clown convention. After much shouting, the owner pacified me, saying he would personally take care of Chief. I handed over the dress whites grudgingly, but not before running a gentle hand across the golden Budweiser on the left breast of the uniform.

"See to it that he looks like he has some dignity Mr. Taylor, or members of his SEAL team and I will be back to visit you."

Letting go of Chief's uniform and hat, I whispered good-bye to my friend.

"My apologies, Mr. Calhoun, it will be done," replied Taylor.

Claire appeared to be doing better, and for that I was grateful. She asked Pepper and me if we would escort her to the funeral, to which of course we said yes. Claire hugged and thanked us both. All other arrangements for the funeral and wake were planned and carried out.

The day had finally came. The day to pay our respects, say good-bye and move on. I found it a difficult thing to do. It was the kind of day Chief loved. Bright blue sky and not a single cloud to be seen anywhere. "Just need a strong wind behind me boy," he would say. Fitting I think, to have a day such as that, to bury him. Personally, I think he would have preferred to just be dumped into the Pacific, a grand party to follow, and maybe a hangover to curse him by. There was no way I could have mentioned this to Claire of course, so like the good little soldier, I carried out what she needed to be done.

Still thinking I was somehow responsible for his death, I realized the futility of constantly second guessing myself. I was able to let that one part of Chief's death go. Deep down I knew it was just one of those things. As much as I hated them, I understood those kind of circumstances happen to good people all the time. I, better than most, understood that. In essence, my good-byes had been said that terrible night when I held him in my arms as he died.

Pepper and I escorted Claire and Ruth, along with her children to the cemetery. The Eulogy had been very trying on everyone. There had been so many well wishers and friends that wanted to say something on Chief's behalf. At that point, the final steps to lay Wallace G. Bennett to rest, were all that remained.

As the priest began his recital, I glanced over at Ruth and watched her hand wiping away a tear. Oh God, how I wanted to just hold her. To comfort her. Then I remembered...

Chief was so proud and happy for his daughter's upcoming wedding. It was all he talked about for two months straight. His excitement was infectious and I found myself hoping all went well for Ruth and her soon-to-be husband, Trevor. Since Trevor had been a good friend of mine, I would have wished nothing but the best for these two anyway.

As a groomsman in the wedding, I was pleased to finally meet Ruth after all I had heard of her. Trevor had been stationed in Florida, and that too was where Ruth resided. They came in a week before the wedding and I had the chance to inspect this woman during rehearsal at the church.

I remembered thinking how pretty she was. An inside beauty as well as outside, made me want to get to know her better. I knew that opportunity would be coming, since Trevor was soon to be transferred back to California. Feeling a stab of guilt for wanting to spend time with her, I brushed it off as looking out for Trevor. I wanted to make sure Ruth wasn't looking to take a ride on my friend. Of course I resided deep down that was not possible. She was, after all, the daughter of Wallace Bennett. No acorn to fall from his tree would be one to take advantage of another.

The wedding came and went without a hitch. They had the honor guard as part of their ceremony and walked proudly under the held high swords as husband and wife. An opportunity to dance with Ruth came, and we talked briefly of this and that. I thought she was intelligent, beautiful and had a great sense of humor, and I wanted to get to know her better. Perhaps, over time, I shall have the pleasure. I thought to myself.

Time did go by, and yes, I did get to see her. More times than I ever thought possible. Was I imagining it, or was she making her presence more frequent whenever I was visiting Chief and Claire? I wasn't sure, but that was how I saw it. If I had been more intuitive, I would have realized that her being at her parents home was actually due to lack of wanting to be at her own. I never realized what had been happening in the home of Trevor and Ruth Phelps.

Three years later, with my own wedding come and gone, I sat talking to a nervous Claire. "Terry, I need a favor. I mean a really big one. You might even consider it two favors."

"Claire, ya know I'd do anythin' for ya. Name it."

"Well, I'm not sure where I want to start, so I'll just do my best. First, all that I speak to you about, must be kept between us. I don't want you speaking to Wallace about any of it."

Holding up three fingers, as in a scout's salute, I said, "I promise."

Claire chuckled, then continued. She knew she could trust me with this or any delicate matter. "Okay Terry, consider that favor number one...Wallace doesn't hear of this. Number two, is that I need you to talk to Ruth. Something's wrong. I'm not sure, but I think Trevor is still hurting her. She makes excuses to not come here or for me not to go to her house. You know that isn't like her at all. We enjoy our time together. I'm not being an excessively protective mother here, I know my daughter."

Sensing my emotions about to go ballistic, I calmly said, "Sure Claire, I'll go see her. I'll letcha know what I find out. And I promise, Chief won't hear about it."

Reaching over to hug me, she whispered, "You know how much I love Janet, but there are some days I wish you had married my Ruth." She always could make me blush.

Since I had the night off, I decided to make the drive to Ruth's house and pop in for a visit. I despised the idea of someone hurting this woman, and certainly didn't mind the out-of-the-way drive to check on her.

Pulling up next to the curb in front of her house, I could see light shining through the curtained windows. Feeling confident that she was home, I had to admit I was a bit nervous at the same time. Nervousness was definitely not something I was familiar with. I stamped out my cigarette and knocked on her door.

Opening it, Ruth obviously wasn't expecting anyone very important or who would know her very well, and cringed when she saw that it was me. I could see the bruises on her neck and arms. Albeit they were fading, but I could tell that the injury to her neck was more substantial and in all likelihood, she had been rendered unconscious because of it. I swung the door open and stepped inside without the benefit of an invitation.

"Give it up Ruth, who did this to you?" I growled. Not one to beat around the bush, I saw no reason to start with her.

David, Ruth's four year old son piped in, "Daddy got mad Uncle Terry, and hit mama."

Kneeling down, I found a matchbox sized police cruiser directly behind David's ear and handed it to him. (A little trick I learned from one of the D.A.R.E. Officers at the station).

"OK pal, thanks for the info, now go play so I can talk to your mama." I watched with a smile as the boy with his new found treasure ran to his room. Hearing a shout of thanks, I set my attention on Ruth.

"So, are you going to tell me what happened?"

"Did my four year old news anchor stutter or speak a foreign language that you may not actually know?"

Her voice had more venom then I thought she was capable of. I actually backed a few steps from her. "Whoa gal, slow down! I only came here..."

Immediately interrupting, still on her soap box, she went on. "And just what the hell are you doing here Terrence Calhoun? I know, I didn't invite you. Did my father send you?"

"No, he did not. He has no idea I'm even here. Your mother sent me. She's concerned and swore me to secrecy about this with your dad. She said nothin' about her suspicions to your father and she's afraid that if she did, he'd do somethin' stupid."

Trying to make up for her blowup, she took a deep breath and asked, "Do you want something to drink? And yes, I know he would do something stupid." Making her way to the kitchen, I could see the tension in her small body.

"Got a beer?" I said with a smile, as I followed her.

"Ummmm...nope, don't keep it in the house, thought you would have remembered that by now Terry." She saw by my smile I did indeed remember, and gave a slight smile of her own. "I have wine, Pepsi or a DR. P." Her voice betrayed her nervousness.

"How about some iced water?" I asked, lowering my voice while peering over her shoulder into the refrigerator.

"I can do that." Ruth appeared to be shaken by my close proximity. She grabbed a container of bottled water for me and reached for the freezer door quickly opening it.

"Hey! You almost hit me with the damn door!"

"Mmmm hmmm, better be careful in this room Terry, all kinds of things in a kitchen that can hurt you." I noticed her eyes turned from their usual soft brown, to black as she got flustered.

"I'm sure there are Ruth, anythin' in particular that you're speakin' of?"

"Just making sure you understand where you are Mister, that's all." The anger seemed to disappear in her as fast as it arose.

She had a perfumed scent that was so light, I felt myself moving closer just to be able to smell it. "I see, sounds like a fair warning to me." Looking deeply into her smoldering eyes, I then spun on my heels and walked out of the kitchen.

"So, you never answered my question Ruth!" I said, over my shoulder.

"I know!"

Watching her enter the room, I admired her body. As far as I could tell, it was flawless. She had always kept up with her appearance, never failing to make my heart beat a bit faster every time I saw her. "Why do you let him do this to you Ruth?"

"You know how he can be Ter. You've seen it plenty of times. I know you didn't think he was more than a lousy drunk. Well, not only that, he's a lousy human being. All I try to do when he comes by, is to keep him calm in front of the kids."

"I could be wrong Ruth, but it doesn't look like it's working anymore." I couldn't help myself, and the sarcasm came heavily. Feeling a fury building up inside of me, I got angrier at the thought of Trevor having his hands on her to intentionally inflict pain.

"He's your friend remember?" Her tone was as sarcastic as my own.

"Indeed. Time for that friendship to end. I gotta run Ruth, I'll talk to Trevor, okay?" I said, making a quick exit to the door. "Call your mom, okay? She's worried about you."

Almost as if she were in a foot race, Ruth tried to catch up to me. With her tiny size dwarfed by my larger mass, she looked up at me. "Be careful Ter, for me and the kids? He will come after me, and I don't want that." She lowered her eyes in shame and a blush spread across her cheeks.

Lifting her chin with a finger, I looked her in the eyes. With a sparkle she'd gotten to know very well, I tried to make her smile. "Don't you fret now, little lady, I'll be my usual tactful self."

"That's what I'm afraid of," she whispered.

With a wink, I said goodnight and took off.

Driving about a mile or so from Ruth's house, I pulled over to use my cell phone. I dialed the number and heard, "Calhoun."

"Hey Pepper, I have a favor to ask ya man."

Pepper laughed, "The thang about it is, I remember the last lil favor I did for ya. I still have to wear a disguise if I wanna go to Florida!"

"I need a locate on someone. A real SOB someone." I explained the who and listed some of the usual hangouts he was known to frequent.

Pepper was quiet a moment. "You sure about this man? You

42

want me to look for Trevor? What has he done to get on your shit list?"

"How 'bout beatin' on innocent women for starters? Yeah, I mean Ruth!"

"Fuck! No problemo brother-man, consider me on it, but do I get to kill him when I find him?"

I was very explicit with my answer. "Just sit on 'em. I don't want 'em to see you or suspect he's being watched. You call me and I'll come runnin.'"

"Roger that, Pepper signin' off!" With that, the phone went dead and I plotted in my mind what I would do to Trevor when I found him. That I would find him was a given, only the when of it was difficult   to   ascertain.

CHAPTER 8
GOODBYE AND HELLO

Two days later the call came in. Just as I was putting my feet up on the couch, the phone rang. "Who is it and whaddaya want?"

"Got 'em!" Pepper replied.

"Where!?" I demanded, pulling on my boots.

"Delvito's. And he's with the ugliest..."

Pepper ended up talking into a phone where no one was on the other end. I got to hear later, how bad my phone manners were. All I knew at that point was I didn't give a rat's ass about courtesy, I had a date at Delvito's.

Tearing out of the house, I shouted to Janet, "I'll be back in a few!" and ran for my truck. Since Janet's car was parked directly behind me, I knew there was no way to maneuver around it.

"Oh well," I said with a shrug, "screw it, if it gets fucked up it's not my fault. I've told her a thousand times not to park behind me!"

Janet raced out of the house as she realized her car was behind my truck. She knew I was going to take it. "Calhoun, we just got that out of the shop from the last time you took it! Your ass is grass if you mess it up again!"

Waving at her, I continued my one-sided argument as to why she shouldn't park behind me. After about twenty-minutes, I turned into the parking lot of Delvito's.

Pulling up beside me, Pepper rolled his window down. "What's the plan dude?" he asked.

"His life expectancy will depend on his attitude." I had that shit-eating grin on my face that told Pepper I couldn't be happier.

Pepper reached inside his jacket and pulled out two cigarettes. Lighting them both, and handing one to me, his thumb rubbed lovingly over the casing of the zippo lighter. As a gift from Chief, it was considered a prized memento. To Pepper, it was his lucky charm.

"Here he comes," Pepper said as he motioned to the door of Delvito's with a big grin. We watched Trevor and his companion walk across the street to where she parked her Volkswagen Jetta. As he kissed her goodnight, Pepper went on to say, "Man, he is with the ugliest..."

As the Jetta sped away, Trevor made his way back to the darkened parking lot behind the bistro. "Oh shit!" I said, cutting him off again. "This couldn't happen better if I planned it myself!"

Quickly jumping out of our vehicles, we quietly jogged across the street. Sending hand commands for what I wanted Pepper to do, he signed his acknowledgment back. We rapidly closed the distance. Pepper circled around and approached Trevor attempting to put his key into the door lock. "'Scuse me pardner, ya wouldn't happen to have a light wouldja?" asked Pepper.

In the same instant, I approached from the reverse angle and moved in. Trevor had no idea what was about to hit him. One thing was certain, he was going to wish he'd never known the names Terry or Pepper. With overpowering speed, I reached for the man I had called friend, turning his body to face me. Within the same span of time, I drew my Emerson CQB folding knife. Flicking my wrist, I extended the blade to its full six inches.

"Terry? Pepper? I thought it was you! What the fuck is this all about?" he asked with uncertainty in his voice.

Again with precise speed, I placed the blade just short of cutting his throat wide open. Pulling the knife away a few inches, I made sure Trevor was well aware of its location. "I want to make sure I have your undivided attention Trev. Is it safe to assume that I do?"

"Please! Terry, what the fuck is goin' on, man?"

Moving closer, Pepper whispered, "The thang about it is, you're in deep shit."

Trevor moved his eyes from Pepper back again to me, not daring to move his head. Visibly shaking, Trevor who usually dressed so impeccably, developed a dark stain that appeared in front of his trousers.

Clenching my hand around his windpipe, Trevor began to wheeze and cough as he tried to inhale the air he so desperately needed. "I want you to know Trev, that if you ever lay so much as one finger on Ruth again, I WILL KILL YOU! Do I make myself clear?"

"Oh God!" rasped Trevor, "I'm sssss...orry." I really think he thought his repentance would buy him mercy, but he had forgotten who he was dealing with.

Squeezing a little tighter, I began to shake Trevor until he lost consciousness. "GOD forgives, Terry doesn't," I snarled, letting his body drop to the pavement.

Looking down at the pile of shit, Pepper realized some of Trevor's windpipe was still inside my fist. "Thought you weren't gonna kill 'em."

"Call 911. Get this asshole some help." With much disgust, I made my way back to Janet's Camaro.

"They're on their way!" shouted Pepper, as he hung up his cell phone.
"Meet you at Dooly's for a quick one?" I asked, while cleaning my hands from the prick who dared to think I would offer forgiveness for this offense.

In the distance we heard sirens, and knew it was our signal to depart.

Pepper threw a thumbs up for approval to my choice for a fine drinking establishment, and to Trevor he said with a chuckle, "Last one there buys the first six rounds!" Checking for any signs of our presence, Pepper was satisfied nothing could be linked to us. Jumping into his truck, he headed out to meet me at Dooley's.

Calling Pepper from my cell phone, I told him to keep a stool warm for me, that I had a quick stop to make first. "Yeah, right, the thang about it is, the last time ya said that, I was waitin' for ya for three days!"

Laughing, I promised my brother I'd be there within the hour. I knew it was late, but had to see Ruth and let her know that Trevor would no longer be a threat to her, or her children. Tapping lightly on the door, I waited for Ruth to answer. When opening the door, the light shone behind her as she stood in the doorway, and I could see her nude body outlined perfectly through her nightgown Averting my eyes, I explained what happened, but not graphically so and assured her that Trevor would no longer be a problem. She moved to hug me and kiss me on the cheek. The only problem was, I didn't know that and as I turned my head, she caught me full on the mouth. For a moment we stood, pressed lips to lips and our eyes wide open. All the thoughts and visions I'd had of this woman rushed through my mind as I closed my eyes, and kissed her the way she was meant to be kissed. Returning it, Ruth wrapped her warm arms around me...

A thunderous boom yanked me back to the funeral. The twenty-one gun salute had begun. Seven men in dress whites were there to show their respect, and each one of them requested the honor to be present for Chief. Twice more the guns fired, then a single trumpeter played taps. My tears flowed freely, I knew it would be the last time I'd cry for my friend, I wouldn't allow it again.

A couple hours later, I stood before Chief's freshly sodded grave. Pepper found me and wrapped an arm around me. Lighting a cigarette, I nonchalantly told Pepper, "Got a call from Allbright. If you're interested, we leave for training in Diego in seven days. He said it would be a vacation for us if we wanted the assignment. I don't know 'bout you bro, but I need some fuckin' R & R. So, you up for some fun?

Like me, Pepper knew we had to move on. We had memories of a much loved man, and we would remember him always. Grinning, he nodded his head in agreement, "The thang about it is, there'd better be women on this vacation."

CHAPTER 9
TRAINING

Looking into the garage at all the gear I rounded up for my assignment, I shook my head with resignation. "Well, I need all this shit." I said quietly to no one. Lowering the tailgate to my pickup, I got ready to load it all up. I glanced up from under my Stetson to see Janet watching me get ready to go. To go God knows where and for God knows how long. Janet's hatred for my assignments was so strong, the poison she would inflict was deadly as any Rattler. We talked late into the night about my other life's work. Janet understood that it was part of who I was before we married. The problem was, to her, I was not the same person. To me, I hadn't changed one iota, nor felt I needed to.

Janet offered me a Mountain Dew and attempted to smile. "Babe, it's just a few months," I said. "You know I have to go." I took a big drink of the Dew and returned it to her.

"I know. Here, gotcha' a little something." From behind her back, she produced a package she had hidden, then handed it to me. It was wrapped and tied delicately with a ribbon. "Just don't open it until after you get on the freeway, okay?"

"Deal," I said, taking the offered present. I stood there with a shit-eating grin. "You know I love surprises."

"Yes, dear, I know." Her grin was as big as my own.

Setting the box on the front seat, I continued loading my supplies. I laughed to myself, as neighbors watched with wonder, and probably a bit of fear as they saw me lifting and moving mass quantities of gun cases. They knew I was a cop, but I think they started to suspect they had a possible Rambo living on their block as well.

My kids were attempting to help with the smaller bags and I had to laugh as Anne, my daughter of four, dragged behind her tiny body, a large duffel. "Hey there little lady, I see you've been workin' on those muscles again!" Throwing me one of her ten million dollar smiles, she set the heavy burden aside as she lifted her arm to show me her muscle. Again I laughed, and together we hoisted the bag onto the truck.

I looked down into her chubby cheeked face and she raised her arms to me. "Pick me up," she said. Reaching down, I scooped her up in my large arms. She gave me a butterfly kiss with her eyelashes to mine, an Eskimo kiss, her nose to mine, and finally, a real kiss with a big wet "Mmmmmmwwwwaaaaah!"

Whispering in her ear I asked, "Are you spoiled?"

"Uh huh." she said, nodding her head up and down looking like one of those bulls you might see in the back of some car with its head bobbing away.

Sliding her down my leg, I set her gently on the ground. "Good!" I said proudly.

I felt her tugging on my pant leg and knelt down to her. "Yes, sugar?"

"Daddy going to work?"

"Yes baby, Daddy has to go to work, but I'll be back soon."

"Promise?"

Pulling on a lock of reddish brown hair that matched my own, I smiled a big smile. "I promise little girl."

From behind me I heard, "You promise?"

Turning toward the voice, I saw Janet holding our two year old son, Simon. "Yes, I promise babe." I looked deeply into her eyes, as if by will alone I could make her believe my words.

Janet handed Simon to me and I tickled him, rubbing my whiskers against his soft toddler chin. The boy laughed and squealed, "More! More!" chuckling, I delivered him back to the waiting arms of his mother.

"Even though you resent him, he loves you very much."

"I know Janet, but now isn't the time to argue about this...again." I knew she heard the tension in my voice, but the words were already said.

Janet gave me one of those I just got you grins. "Whose arguing?" she asked, as she stepped back to let me finish the rest of my packing.

Once done, I handed out last minute hugs to the kids, and then it was Janet's turn. She hugged me tight, not wanting to let go. "Come home," she whispered. "Your family loves you and needs you." She moved to kiss me and in her best Terry impersonation, she grabbed a fistful of my shirt and in a gruff voice said, "If you don't come back, I'm gonna hunt you down, pull your eyes out of their sockets and skull fuck you! You got me Mister?"

Snapping to attention, I saluted her. "Ma'am, yes ma'am!"

"At ease!" Janet barked, then with a quick kiss and I love you, she scooped up the kids and hurried into our home. Janet refused to watch me pull away. She didn't want the last memory of me to be driving away.

Adjusting my Stetson for the setting sun, I lifted the tailgate and banged it shut. I saw how much the truck sagged from the extra weight and shook my head. I knew Pepper had as much, if not more cargo for our little vacation than I did. Laughing to myself, Fuck it, it's my truck, he'll have to deal with it. Slipping my black ice mirrored Oakley's back onto my face, I climbed into the cab of my jet black Dodge Ram Club. As I turned the key to start her up, I looked up toward the house one last time. I watched the blinds to my living room window swing back to their closed position. Nodding, I dropped the truck into drive and pulled away. Checking the G-shock on my wrist I saw it was 1840 hours. Damn, I hate getting shit from Pepper when I'm late. I thought to myself.

My big Dodge merged effortlessly onto the 215 Freeway. Traffic was light and commuters were home getting ready to sit down with their families for dinner. That beautiful tint of early evening sky was fanned out with pinks and purples and orange. A light mist began to coat the windshield and I used the wipers to clear the view. The sun began its dip behind Mt. Rubidoux and I couldn't help but admire the beauty of it. Only for a moment did I allow myself that luxury. Changing lanes, I prepared to exit to the 60 Freeway heading toward Moreno Valley. As I made the lane change, my cell phone rang. I placed it in the cradle and pushed the send button. "Calhoun!" I answered.

"Shit, am I on speaker phone? You know I hate speaker phone."

"Tough shit Pepper, whatcha want?"

"You still coming or what?"

I knew exactly where the conversation was headed, the little prick loved to give me a hard time. "I'm on my way."

"Uh huh, before Christmas would be nice."

I cut him off still hearing his laughter in the back ground. With a grin I thought, go fuck yourself. Turning up the radio, I hummed to the song, Much Too Young To Feel This Damn Old. Lighting a Marlboro, I dropped the windows while thinking how much the song paralleled my feelings at that moment. I contemplated the words to the song and agreed, "Yep, I am too young to feel this damn old."

I finally pulled into Peppers neighborhood. That in itself was reason to laugh 'cause there was no neighborhood. Pepper was it! He owned a modest mobile home on some not so modest land. Pepper was shrewd with his property, but not, unfortunately, with much else. He had found "the sweetest patch of yard that money could buy," or so he bragged. Truth be told, I was very proud of my little brother, but he really needed some work in other areas. Christ, like I didn't? I had to agree with Pepper, it was beautiful and relaxing. The perfect place to maintain a hiatus from our line of work. There were hundreds of trees. Ponds, animals and flowers flourished throughout the property. Anything one would want from nature resided out his front door.

As I entered the lane he lived off, I spied Sharon, Pepper's sometimes off, always on girlfriend. She loved him so much and could forgive him any transgression. Deep down I always thought she was too good for him, that she deserved better. I love Pepper, but didn't care for the way he treated this sweet, loving woman. Waving hello, she motioned for me to stop. "Hey darlin, whatcha doin' here." I asked.

Even though the wind blew her blond hair across her face, I could still make out the saddened look in her eyes. "I just wanted to say good-bye to you guys."

She never lifted her eyes to meet mine and I knew what she was going through. I climbed out of my Dodge and put out my cigarette with my size thirteen, black lace up combat boots. "What do you want to know?" I asked her.

"Where are you going and when will you back?"

"What else do you want to know?" I thought a little joke might pull out a smile, but I played that hand wrong.

Looking up at me with defiance in her eyes, it unfortunately didn't last long as they filled with her tears. "I am so tired of being kept out of the loop," she said as tears rolled down her cheeks.

Peering into her green eyes, I told her, "You know I can't tell you that Sharon. But I promise you after the trainin's over and we get settled in, we will call. It's all I can tell you."

Sharon smiled, because she knew I would not lie to her, although she may have suspected I had in the past to protect her from something Pepper had done.

"C'mon missy, climb in, I'll take ya up the driveway."

She shook her head no. "Thanks anyway Ter, I need some time to get my shit together."

Nodding my understanding, she watched me as my truck rumbled up the drive. I peered into the rearview mirror and watched her wiping at the tears she could not stop on behalf of love for my brother. Pressing my palm against the steering wheel, the air horns blared, announcing my arrival to my step brother. I turned off the motor and stepped out of the truck. "Pepper!! Get your worthless, goat fuckin' ass out here!!"

Pepper charged and body checked me. The two of us rolled around on the ground as he tried to overpower me. Sitting on top of my chest, he musta thought he was the king cock. "'Gotcha this time, ya old fart!" He said with a smirk.

"Pepper, let me ask you something. That thing you feel in your back? You don't really think that's a hard on do you?" He looked me in the eye, and knew he was fucked again.

Instantly freezing, he peered behind and down his shoulder. He realized his brother one-upped him again, as he saw the .45 caliber Glock pointed directly at his kidney.

"The thang about it is, if you weren't so much bigger'n me, we'd be scrappin' right now." He laughed as he climbed off of me and with extended hand to me said, "C'mon old timer, get up."

Taking the offered help with a big grin, we both looked over at Sharon as she made her way across the large front yard. She smiled at our antics, but knew what a dangerous combination us two boys were. Pepper met her and wrapped his arms around her. I couldn't make out the conversation, but heard her last words to him.

"I love you God dammit!" She then hightailed it for the house.

Shaking my head, I was thinking the scene looked very familiar. "I think it's in the water bro, Janet did the same damn thing."

Pepper laughed and was in a great mood. "Good thing we don't drink water, huh Terry?"

He and I began the task of adding his shit to my already full pickup truck. When the last of the gear was stowed away and the tailgate slammed shut, we fastened down the tarp to cover our precious cargo. Pepper wiped his hands as if he just completed a very dirty task.

"Well, Ter," he went on to say, "I'm ready for some southern exposure, let's get the hell outta here!

CHAPTER 10
SAN DIEGO WAY

"Hey! Turn this up!" Said Pepper, wanting to hear his favorite song, Highway To The Danger Zone at somewhere along the lines of the 200 decibel range. Our need for speed was always heightened by this song, and tonight was no exception. I never hesitated and reached for the volume, turning the knob with a quick twist. "Yeah! That's the ticket!" he shouted, with a smile as big as the whole outdoors.

As I laid into the go pedal and the speedo tickled the century mark Pepper's singing got louder and worse, as if he thought the louder it was the better it was. "Hey Pep"! I yelled straining my vocal cords to get his attention. I laughed to myself, the windows are down, every coon dog in a fifty mile radius must be howling right about now.

I leaned forward in my seat to push the cigarette lighter in and as I sat back up I saw him. "SHIT"! I said loudly with concern in my voice, that made Pepper stop dead in his tracks and look straight at me, "What"? He asked as he scanned picking him up as the red and blues went on.

"Well fuck me runnin'" Pepper sing songed in his Mississippi accent. "Hey!, he spun in his seat and asked, 'you want me open the nitrous bottle"? As we came up on the next exit I caught a glimpse of a self-service gas station with an attached car wash. "I've got a better idea."

Pepper understood my drift and sang, "I like it, I love it, I want some more of it!"

"There should be a shitload of quarters in the ashtray!" I said, as I sawed the wheel and screeched into the gas station.

"Got 'em!" Pepper scooped up a handful of the silver coins.

As we pulled up to the car wash, I fed the hungry machine and drove in. Almost immediately, the soap was covering the truck. Pepper and I watched in utter amazement as the "chippy" cruised by. "I can't believe that fuckin' worked! Remind me to use that in my book!" I said with a chuckle. Turning on the wipers momentarily, I checked on the status of the police car. We watched as it made another pass, turned off its red and blues, then headed back for the Freeway.

"High five on that mother!" said Pepper defiantly.

Leaning back in my seat, I reached for a cigarette just as the rinse cycle finished and eased the truck out of the wash bay. Damn good thing we remembered to use the tarp to cover our load. The truck glided out the drive way and I hauled ass for the 5 Freeway. Water streamed toward the back of the truck as we picked up speed. After reaching the 5, I raced for the 8 Freeway and cranked up the radio again.

"We're about thirty-five minutes out now Ter!"

I didn't acknowledge that bit of information but squinted at the speedometer. "Hmmm, gonna have to do better than one twenty to make up for our interruption."

"You go boy!" Pepper shouted. In nothing flat, we were positioning ourselves onto the 8 Freeway. "Terry, it's only twenty minutes to the interchange!"

"Turn on the transponder Pep, don't want to surprise anyone with our presence." I smiled, thinking of Ponce waging his own little war on a trespassing truck.

We exited the freeway and followed the directions from the email. they were very specific and while we were smart-asses we weren't stupid. We found the turn off onto a well maintained graded, three car wide dirt road and almost as we made the first sweeping turn, out of the blue, a Porsche appeared in my rearview mirror.

Before I could say anything of it to Pepper, it blew my V-8 out of the water. "Fuck that Terry! You ain't gonna take that shit from Phil are ya!?"

"Too close for missiles, switch to guns!" I ordered. I couldn't see a god damned thing with all the dirt Phil roosted as he went by in a full drift.

Pepper knew exactly what I was referring to and reached under the passenger seat to remove a flare gun. Positioning himself out the window, he took aim and shouted, "Fire in the hole!" The flare took off in a wild spiral toward the 914 and we laughed as we watched Phil try to keep control of his precious car.

I dropped the hammer on the big truck, fishtailing the ass end out in the dirt returning the roost favor, while Pepper, still hanging out the window was yelling at Phil, trying to taunt him. "Hungry Phil? Eat your fuckin' import!!" He sent a hand signal to Phil, with his middle finger doing the talking. As we thundered by the out of control German sports car, we looked out the back window to see Phil struggling to get his car to do his bidding.

When we turned to focus our attention to the view in front of us, it was too late to stop, and we were about to crash through the fence that surrounded Ponce's land. "Shit! Pepper, hold on!! We're goin' in and we are VSF!" Even as the barb wire was being ripped off its posts, the screams and threats of the guards went unheard from the roar of the engine and blasting of the stereo.

"Very seriously fucked!" Pepper added.

Jerking the wheel of the Dodge, I made an effort to evade Phil's advancements and hoped I'd miss Ponce's land mines. Phil's car finally spun to a halt, but not before his front tire shredded from the barbed wire. Pepper jumped out of the truck in a cloud of dust so thick, I couldn't see beyond the hood.

I slammed the brakes in an attempt to keep from crashing into Phil. Knowing that Pepper was no longer in the cab, I prayed I didn't end up running him over or smashing into Phil's car. Squeezing my eyes shut and bracing for what I thought would be impending impact with something, I finally slid to a stop. I let out a long low breath realizing I didn't hit anyone or anything.

To Peppers surprise, Phil was already waiting for him with weapon drawn. As he pointed it at Pepper, he was yelling at the top of his lungs. "Who the hell taught you clowns how to drive!?"

Slipping out of the truck, I crouched down as low as I could, and made my way to the front end. I jumped up with both hands full and what I had in them was extremely lethal. Of course, whenever dealing with Phil, one always maintained their cool. "Well, howdy Phil! How the hell are ya?"

Phil smiled and the three of us re-holstered our weapons. I told Phil, "Good plan, bad execution," laughing all the way of course.

"The thang about it is," piped in Pepper, "you need a bigger vehicle."

Phil just laughed at us two yahoos. This was one of his little pet names for us both. "Yeah, yeah, you guys gonna just stand there or can you give me a hand with this tire?"

We Yahoo brothers glanced at each other and began clapping at Phil. "Shit, you two are sooooo fuckin' funny." Removing his perfectly tailored suit jacket, he carefully set it on the seat in his car. "Either of you comedians have a flashlight?"

The blinding light of ten mercury bulbs flashed on in an instant. "Someone ask for a light?" a voice asked from the darkness. The three of us drew our weapons until we realized who the voice belonged to and saw the man emerge from the shadows.

"I was gonna say, I hope you own the patent rights to that flashlight!" smirked Phil.

Ponce, who stood in full view, had only seconds before been

standing completely undetected in the shadows. We all exchanged embraces. It had been quite some time since the four of us had been together. Ponce transmitted something in his radio and several seconds later, three very large men disengaged themselves from the darkness. To Phil and us Calhoun brothers, he said, "C'mon boys, let's leave that for the hired help. Hugo! See to it that the vehicles are brought up to the main house after you repair that tire."

"Sir, yes Sir!" Saluted Hugo. The man was left saluting the desert, then turned to his cohorts. "You heard him men, let's get this POV repaired on the double!"

CHAPTER 11
TEN HUT

After the long walk through the compound, Ponce led us up the stairs into the foyer of the house. Pepper whispered to Phil, "Dontcha' just love the understated home?" I nudged Pepper trying to signal him to shut up. Pepper and I had visited Ponce's home before, and normally we never could pass up on giving his ass shit for his uncanny style in decor.

One always had the impression of being in either a resort or a prison when in Ponce's home. On that particular day, I had the distinct feeling I walked into a personal version of Attica and God only knew who the fuckin' warden was. So, I was there for the duration, or whenever I deemed it time to depart from that palatial hole in the desert.

Ponce waved an arm to motion to an older man standing in fatigues at the foot of the stairs. "Show the Calhouns' and Mr. Hanlon to their respective rooms," I may as well have had a mouthful of dick for as quiet as I was when he said it. I know Pepper had to about shit his drawers thinking I would say something in return. So I just looked Ponce straight in the eye and swallowed it. Believe me, I know now, why some women have that difficulty. Ponce stopped in mid stride and turned to face us. "Gentlemen, chow is in one hour." He couldn't seem to help himself and squinted at me a moment longer than he had to. I suppose it was his way of saying, "not bad, ya learned quick on when to keep your cocksucker shut." He then turned smartly on his heel and disappeared around the corner.

I whispered to Pepper, "He reminds me of Higgins", "who"?, "you know, Magnum PI"? I had to grab Pepper and cover his mouth in fell swoop as he fuckin lost it and Ponce was still well within earshot.

As we were making our way up the oak staircase, I paid close attention to the old man who was leading the way. I noticed as we reached the top step, that he wasn't even out of breath. Watching this man's gait, his movements and the sinewy muscles under his tight T-shirt, led me to believe he took care of himself and was probably a lot more dangerous than he appeared.

We approached one of the rooms and the old man stopped and handed Phil a single key. In a monotone voice he told him to enjoy his stay. "Yeah, right, six weeks at the lovely Waldorf Astoria," I thought to myself. Next, it was time for Pepper and me to be escorted to our room. He led us to the end of the hall, handed us two keys and pointed to the last door to the right.

We entered our quarters, and quickly set about the task of searching it. We were looking for any type of television camera or electronic surveillance equipment that the "Warden" might be trying to infiltrate us with. Our search was complete and we were empty handed, Pepper was starting to get frustrated. "The thang about it is," he went on to say, "we're gonna have to search this room every day. He's had all this time to set these rooms up, why wouldn't he have done it by now?"

"Think about it Pepper, the first thing we're gonna do when we get in this room is search it. I don't know what they have planned for us, as far as this training goes. But you figure if they're gonna be runnin' our asses off for ten hours a day, the last thing we're gonna be in the mood for is takin' a shit, much less making a sweep. That way we don't talk about anythin' that doesn't pertain to any of their business. We just have to make sure that whoever's doin' the peekin,' doesn't figure out we're on to 'em."

I walked across the room thinking I could use a tar bar. As I opened the French doors to the veranda, Pepper anticipated my need and tossed me my pack of Marlboros. Firing up two, I handed one off to him and turned to look out over the spacious ranch.

The peaceful silence was broken as a shrieking alarm sounded off inside the room. From the speaker above the beds an unfamiliar voice asked that there be no smoking inside the quarters. Pepper took a deep drag and blew the smoke directly into the detector, and in his usual wise-ass way said, "No problem dude, whatever you say".

Pepper ambled out to meet me on the balcony, and an idea hit me, like a face first jump in the ocean from two-hundred feet. I snatched another cigarette out of the pack in Pepper's pocket. "Hey man, you nervous?" Asked Pepper. "You haven't even finished the one you've got in your mouth."

"Give me some string or something Pepper, lift up your T-shirt, you got some rope or something?"

"Yeah, sure, I got some thread." I took the strand that Pepper had torn from his shirt, took the cigarette from Pepper's mouth and tied all three together with the thread. "What, you can't hold three cigarettes in your mouth without thread?"

"Watch this, if my theory is correct..." I flipped the cigarette over the edge onto the ground, seconds later, two armed guards appeared as if in response to an intrusion. Pepper was standing there with his mouth open, like I just ran out naked singing the Star Spangled Banner. The two guards looked straight up at us and we did a fine display of our best Forrest Gump wave. The guards shook their heads in disgust and walked back to their duty station. Couldn't help chucklin' at Mutt and Jeff as they made their way back to whatever fuckin' rock they slithered out from underneath.

Pepper trailed after me into the bedroom. As he began to speak, I raised my right hand in a clenched fist signaling dead stop. We moved into the bathroom, closing the door behind us. Pepper turned on the water in both sinks while I reached in to turn the shower on. All movements made, were in complete silence. Standing in the middle of the spaciously ornate tiled bathroom, and having to speak from mouth to ear, I confessed to Pepper, "We've obviously underestimated our host. Somebody is definitely watchin' and listenin' to everythin' we say. I figure it'll only be a couple of hours before the sensitivity on the thermal imaging will be reconfigured. Otherwise we're gonna have some fun smokin' and droppin' cigarettes all night long."

63

The steam rising from the shower had fogged up the glass. Pepper whispered in my ear, "You couldn't have turned on the cold water?"

I turned him around to face the mirror, which had two distinct shapes which refused to submit to the fog. I whispered back into Pepper's ear, "Here's one reason we couldn't find the cameras".

Pepper traced the outline on the glass. "I'll fix that later. Well, we might as well take our showers since the water is runnin,' then get ready to eat."

We walked out of the bathroom, leaving the shower running, and Pepper turned my attention to the metal lockers next to each of the beds. He pointed to the one on the left and told me it was mine. I stepped in closer and noticed my name tag on the slot. I pulled up on the stainless steel handle and opened the door. "I guess they want us to wear these while we are here." I stripped off my clothes and made my way back to the bathroom. "I'll be out in a sec."

Pepper called out to me, "Leave it runnin!"

I finished with the shower then traded places with Pepper, who had just finished brushing his teeth. "Your turn bro"" I told him. I quickly brushed my teeth and lacking the ability to shave, headed into the bedroom to get dressed. I noticed Pepper had laid out my clothes for me.

"Thanks Ma!" I shouted, but I doubted he heard me holler at him in the bathroom. I just couldn't resist saying it. I dressed in the supplied black fatigues and white T-shirt with my name stenciled on the back. I scanned the room, feeling as if something were missing, but I couldn't quite put my finger on it. I grabbed a pack of cigarettes off the table and before I headed outside, I lowered the temperature of the cool air blowing out of the wall-mounted air conditioning unit.

With the sliding glass door open, I heard the shower shut off. As Pepper returned to the bedroom, he was shouting at me. "You did that just to make my nipples hard!" He gestured to the air conditioner with a smile on his face.

"Yeah well, you know how I get when I don't get any for a few hours."

Pepper meandered to his locker, opened it and withdrew his uniform. "Ok brother, its time for a sit down." Pepper looked me straight in the eye, showing his concern and seriousness in the situation we were in.

"No shitter time huh?"

"Remember our deal?" He sat back in a chair pulling his socks on.

"Which one?"

"The one about you goin' into the private sector for training and me goin' into the military for training."

"Yeah, what about it?"

"This is my world you're in now, everything here is gonna be based on military training." I listened intently to everything Pepper said "In order to survive this program you're gonna hafta follow my footsteps. Do as I say, do what I do and remember above all else, it's "Sir, yes Sir!" Always." I nodded my head in understanding. Pepper stood up, pulled his pants up and buttoned them. He secured his web belt and looked around. "You ready?"

"Lets do it!" I stood and we both headed for the door.

Phil was just at the top of the stairs when we slammed the door shut to our room. "Well, if it isn't the Yahoo twins."

We didn't rise to his bait and kept moving down the hall toward the stairs. Pepper scanned the foyer as we made our way down the spiraling, lightly stained, oak staircase. We were all led to the mess hall by the same elder gentleman who showed us to our rooms earlier.

The mess area was about eighteen feet long by twenty feet wide. The tables looked as though they were bought used on government closeout. Even the silverware and trays were standard military issue. I heard Pepper whisper to Phil, "This brings back memories huh, Phil?" Pepper was looking more and more as if he were at home, instead of a major training session.

"What the fuck have I gotten myself into now?" I said softly, hoping no one heard it, but I knew Pepper probably did.

CHAPTER 12
MY NEW LIFE

As I was surveying the dining room Phil jabbed at me. "C'mon, I'm hungry."

I fell in behind Pepper and Phil and leaned forward to whisper in my brothers ear. "I'm right behind you."

Pepper nodded in apparent amusement, loving every bit of it and knowing he had his older brother by the short and curlies. He just grinned that upper hand grin. "Ya don't have to git that close."

A deep resonating voice broke through the chow time chatter. "Take all you want, but you better eat what you take!" I had heard that before, but that's only in the movies, right? I turned to see who had boomed out those words and stared in disbelief. Pepper kicked me from under the table. I mouthed the word, "What?" as my attention was shifted to him.

His eyebrows furrowed and his face was contorted as he was silently chastising me for staring. I had a feeling something really bad was about to happen. I felt the hairs on my neck raise up in anticipation of it. Again I mouthed, "What?" to Pepper, but it was to no avail. He looked down at his tray and would have nothing to do with me. He was trying to avert attention from either of us, but it was too late. We were way beyond attention getting. We had become a full blown focal point.

The DI who had been making his rounds was standing behind me and I never heard him come near me. All of a sudden a bellow came from my blind side. "MAGGOT!! IS THERE A PROBLEM!?"

Without a blink of an eye or pass of a heartbeat, Pepper was on the ball, "SIR, NO SIR!" Phil never missed a beat and kept shoveling at his food. Anything to keep from bringing any wrath upon himself. He could've been eating dog shit and it would have made no difference. Pepper's eyes rolled back in his head as if to say,

"Oh shit", and yet once more I mouthed, "what?" The DI was now standing so close to me, I could feel the heat radiating off his body.

The Drill Instructor stood about 5'10". He had broad shoulders and looked like an inverted pyramid. In the middle of all of this sat his head. I swear he bore a striking resemblance to that red dog from the beer commercials, more than a man. I couldn't tell if he had a neck, his head just sorta turned, more than swiveled. His flat top and whitewalls were checked by scars and flecked with gray. His skin was dark and wrinkled from too many years in the desert sun.

Pepper was trying desperately to get my attention. I found this DI so amusing, I really didn't pay Pepper too much mind. He may as well have been talking to a fuckin' wall. He kept mouthing, "Sir, sir...you need to say sir!" Just as that brilliant light bulb went ding in my shit sifter, it was too late. Red Dog had me by the nape of the neck and was lifting me from my chair. I couldn't believe the strength in the man. His arms were the size of redwoods and I was caught in his grip.

"SIR! YOU LOW-LIFE, SHIT-EATING, HUMAN FUCK STAIN!! HE IS TRYING TO TELL YOU, YOU FORGOT TO SAY SIR!!"

To say he raised his voice was an understatement. It was closer to thunder than a human voice and it got my attention immediately. The DI was yelling so hard it was actually making my hair move on top of my head. This was nothing like the police academy. I always figured Pepper was telling one of his UN-fucking believable tales when he spoke of basic training.

Then it happened. When that light bulb went off, it was just the beginning. The rest of me had to follow and I knew what had to be done to succeed, this was not for fun and games. This was going to take concentration, dedication and a level head. This was going to be a challenge, and with a Calhoun, failure was not an option. I stood frozen. The smirk on my face now long gone. I stood straight, tall and took a deep breath. "SIR, NO SIR!!" I answered.

"Sit down soldier!"

"SIR, THANK YOU SIR!!" I took my place back at the table, feeling, to say the least, more humble, which as a Calhoun, was not an easy task. Again I was forced to swallow, but hey, that was starting to get a lot easier. Pepper once again kicked me. "Now what?" I whispered. He gestured with his head toward the front of the room.

"Somethins' up," he whispered back. Richard Allbright, the DI and two men in suits were huddled together in some kind of pow wow. "Every time the stripes assemble in the mess during chow, it means somethins' up."
"Good or bad somethin'?"

He just shrugged his shoulders with indifference. "Just...somethin'."

"Officer on Deck! Atteeeeeenshun!! OK, listen up!" All the men are standing at attention and I was one of them. "At ease!" In unison, we all stood at parade rest. I couldn't see who was barking all the orders, and frankly, I didn't give a rat's ass. I was mirroring Pepper's every move and was too focused on him to care. One thing that struck me as a point of interest, was that all thirteen men were dead quiet and stayed that way. The silence was broken by the red haired man, whom I had affectionately named Red Dog. "Fall out for inspection!" Red Dog barked.

Off to the side of the mess hall was a pair of exit doors. They were wide open and the twelve other men and myself were scrambling to get outside. As I reached the door, I was greeted by the cool desert air. After what I had been through in a short period of time with just Red Dog, the air was refreshing. But I knew what to expect. After years of playing in the desert on my off-time, the temp could reach one hundred fifteen to one hundred twenty during the day and after the sun went down, the mercury would plummet into the thirties.

Our group assembled outside on the cement patio. Each man in the group extended his left arm to the shoulder of the person standing next to him. I was next to the last in line, Pepper was to my right. I followed his direction and extended my left arm out. I was met with a soft, yet firm something with the back of my hand. Still moving the line left, I flipped my hand over and with my palm thought I might give the heavy weight next to me some shit.

Before I could turn my head to see whose chain I was yanking, a soft female voice whispered in my ear. "So, what do I owe you for that?"

I snapped my head left and immediately snatched my hand back. "What the fuck?"

"Don't stop now, I was just getting into it."

I could feel my face grow red and warm. The kind of embarrassment that burns all the way to the tips of your ears. OK, so I was feeling like a dick. But hey, Calhouns recover quickly. I put on a sweet smile and regained my composure, and told her, "Well, we could finish this later.......?" I was prodding her for a name.
"Bina."

"OK, Bina." Just then, Chief Warrant Officer Red Dog made his appearance. A loud, "Officer on Deck!" was heard, and the whole group stood at attention. I finished her off with a, "By the way, you've got nice tits. As Red Dog made his way down the line, Bina, who I again underestimated pinched my ass. It wasn't much, but enough to force me to jump and once again become a focal point.

Pepper was breathing, "Shit.....", under his breath and I'm doing all I can to keep still. So, under my breath I hissed out, "Bitch."

"Mmmm hmmmm don't you ever forget it." She whispered with a heavy accent that was familial.

Red Dog stopped in front of me. Oh gee, a fuck me surprise there. He stood there looking me up and down as I stared straight ahead. I was so tight and so frozen, that you couldn't drive a needle

70

into my ass with a nine pound hammer. "Haven't we met maggot?"

"SIR, YES SIR!"

"Calhoun, step out!"

I took one long step out from the rest of the line.

Pepper was holding his breath as he saw Red Dog look his way. "Is your name Calhoun?"

"SIR, YES SIR!!"

"I SAID OUT!! ARE YOU FUCKIN' DEAF!? I swear to god his voice ran up six more octaves, and I thought he would surely burst a vein.

"SIR, NO SIR!" Quickly, Pepper made his way to stand next to me. Wishing I'm sure, that he had no possible kinship to me.

With sarcasm as thick as cum the Dog started in on us. "I have an idea! Every time either one of you fuck's up, slips behind, jerks off or generally just irritates me, you will both pay! DO I MAKE MYSELF CLEAR!?"

"SIR, CRYSTAL, SIR!!" We shouted together.
"Fall in pond scum!" We both stepped back without looking, hoping our fellow members would step aside for us. Fortunately for us they did, and we were once again standing back with the others, looking good and standing tall.

Pepper hissed at me, "Fuck you Row, she damn well better swallow." I nodded my 10-4.

The Chief moved back to the front of the line and Pepper and I could finally breath again. Judging by Red Dog's voice, the focal point was elsewhere. "What the hell are you shit grinnin' at, Cumspot!?" The Dog shouted.

71

"SIR, NOTHING, SIR!!"

I didn't care who was getting an ass reaming, I was not about to turn my head to find out.

Red Dog was on a roll. With his thick, bone twisted mass he called a finger, he pointed it right at the mans face. "You, will not laugh at your new comrades. You are assembled here 'cause someone thinks highly enough of you to do the job at hand." Now he was starting to pace. I was beginning to feel something deep inside myself. I wasn't sure what it was exactly, but it was there nonetheless.

"I am here," continued the Dog, "to assist you in bringing that, and all of your other hidden qualities to the surface! As far as I'm concerned every shit for brains one of ya is a worthless puddle of spilled fuck!" His pacing continued and his tempo slowly increased. I was really getting charged up! "It is my job to fix what nature fucked up. What I mean by this, is you are not perfect, but I am! And I will make you better than me or kill you trying! Is that understood!?"

"Sir, yes sir!" You could tell all of us in unison were feeling that charge!

The Dog's voice boomed even louder, "I CAN'T HEAR YOU!!"

All together in cadence we thundered back, "SIR, YES SIR!"

Tomorrow is an easy day for you sand lice. You will fall out for PT right here at 0500! From there you will spend most of your day in class! Diiiiiiiismissed!!"
"HOOYAH!!"

Pepper and I lingered behind the others to stand by Bina I reached into my left cargo pocket and pulled out a pack of cigarettes and a black zippo lighter.

I started to laugh out loud for a moment, and Pepper wanted in on my secret. "Whasso funny?" He asked.

"I was just thinkin' about who gave me this lighter." I was rubbing my thumb across it as if it were my magic lamp. "Trevor gave me this at his wedding." Pepper shared my amusement in that particular memory.

"Whatever happened to him Row?"

"Couldn't tell ya. Ruth said she never heard from him again." I took a long draw from and dropped it in the coffee can that had been painted bright red and stenciled with the word BUTTS across it.

I leaned against the wall, making eye signals to Pepper, to just relax and leave the talking to me. Bina stood casually between the two of us. Her 5'7" fit figure accented her olive skin. Her dark hair was pulled back into a pony tail, but I figured it was probably shoulder length when allowed to be down. She wore no makeup and had only a small gold ball earring in each lobe. Her neck was long and thin and sinewed with muscle. I knew firsthand she had small, firm tits. Her hips and lower body were partially hidden by the oversized but well fitted tactical pants. Her outward appearance would put her in her thirties. Anything other than a casual glance however, would betray her. My guess placed her more around forty-two or forty-three. Her eyes gave her away. I looked deep into that gateway of her soul, beyond her green guardians. What I saw there surprised me. Part of her seemed scared and another part anxious. I couldn't tell if she was hiding anything or not. Her past perhaps? I made a mental note to keep an eye on her.

Pepper just can't stand to have a nice looking woman so near and not talk to her, "So, what's a nice girl like you doin' in a shit pile like this?"

I lit another cigarette and she held out two fingers toward me, ignoring Peppers line. "May I?" She asked.

"Certainly," I said, and handed her the pack. Without

extinguishing the flame, I handed her the lighter.

She returned it with a, "Thank you."

"Israeli?" I was trying to pick up on her accent.

"Yesss. How didzyou know"?

"I have a friend who was Mossad."

"Ahhh, I see. And You? From where do you come? Wait! Do not tell me. Let me guess. Hmmmmm..... New York, no?

"Damn, she's good, huh Rowdy?" Pepper didn't quite catch what the drift was, but I figured I would clue him in later.

"Indeed." I had one eyebrow raised and cautiously continued. "I think it's simply amazing."

"Mr. Calhoun, you will find I am a woman of many talents." "your brosser does not sound as you, deep sous"? I could almost hear her say south but her accent just wouldn't let it through, "Louisiana".

I nodded to her and leaned my face near her as if I were going to kiss her cheek. Instead I keep going and move to her ear, and whispered, "David amar li." (So David has told me).

Bina flashed a nervous smile to the two of us, and hurriedly excused herself. Pepper was trying to WTF me. I just told him I would tell him a little later. I blinked my eyes upward to where Red Dog was standing on the balcony. Pepper winked his understanding and we vacated the area and headed back to our quarters.

CHAPTER 13
LADIES NIGHT

We entered our quarters to find that our belongings had been brought to us by Hugo and Company. We ran a quick check and saw that nothing was missing. Pepper reached into one of many bags he had for his little tricks, and retrieved a tin of Lincoln Bootblack. (That's shoe polish for you civilians following along) He flashed a quick smile and headed to the bathroom. "I'm gonna take care of our little guest problem on the mirror," he said.

As he walked to the head, I noticed some reading material that had been conveniently left on top of each locker. That really irked me that we had someone coming in without our permission. "Hmmmm, think we just might have to set a few mousetraps to make sure fingers aren't goin' where they shouldn't be," I said to myself. I picked up the booklet that was left on my locker, and read the cover. Field Ops training I leafed through the manual quickly and whistled loudly at some of its contents.

"Fuckin A! This should be interesting"! I said out loud. "Who has to know this shit, really"? I asked in a somber tone. "I mean part of this includes long distance shooting, WTF Pep, were bodyguards for fucks sake" my tone unchanged.

I was still reading through my copy as I walked into the bathroom to show Pepper. I looked up to see him putting the finishing touches on the mirror. He had blackened out the areas we had determined the cameras were peek-a-booing us. "Whatcha' think? He asked, as he motioned to the two black circles on the wall-to-wall mirror over the double vanity. He then pointed to the upside down arch under the blackouts with great pride. "This way I have a happy face to wake up to." He was referring to my fuck you in the morning demeanor. I flipped him off, those one finger salutes are quite the catchall for what ails you. He blew me a kiss in return. Sometimes, I really did worry about that boy.

Pepper began to unpack more of his gear, taking stock in what he had, and what good it would serve us. What he pulled out first, was an Ultra High Frequency Counter. "The better to find out who is listening to you with my dear," he said. I knew what it was, but my electronics was not as polished as his were, and he knew it. He extended the antenna and turned the unit on. Slipping the earphone into his ear, he set about the business of sweeping the room for bugs. Not the six-legged variety mind you, but the kind that hear everything you say. Well, we couldn't have that, now could we?

I watched Pepper doing his thing, when my eyes stopped on the package Janet had given me before I left. I got off my bed to pick it up, and set it on a rectangular table near the sliding glass doors. Pulling up a chair to it, I sat down smiling, just looking at it. Janet knew how much I loved surprises. I ran a finger across the blue silver foil wrapping and reached for the small card tucked under the black ribbon. It simply read: "PLEASE KEEP IN TOUCH. I LOVE YOU, J."

Pepper was starting to be more interested in my package than his extermination job, and gestured toward it. "What is it?"

"I don't know yet, since when have you known me to be able to see through objects dumb shit?" I tore away the paper and it revealed a cardboard box. As I opened it, I could see the styrofoam peanuts protecting its cargo. I tipped it gently and shook the peanuts out of the way, and my eyes opened wide. "Jeezus Christ, Janet got me a laptop!" I had been wanting one for some time and never got around to buying it. I unzipped the cover case and pulled out my treasure. There was a post-it-note attached to the top of the computer: "It's pre-loaded, just like the one at home."

Pepper was peering over my shoulder, watching me and looking back to my new toy. "Ya know, it works way better if you turn it on," he chided, "just like a woman."

I looked up at him and shook my head. The boy definitely had pussy on the brain, and I thought I was bad. "Mmmm hmmm, Pep, I know. About the 'puter and the woman."

He was looking at the mess I was starting to make all over the table, and he gently began to sort through it all. "Whatcha' need Row, is a modem card. This one will look like a credit card with a square hole in its outer edge. It won't be very big." We were both sorting through the peanuts, and the papers that spilled out with them. "I got it!" He called out happily, "You just slide it in here." Pepper took the card and turning the PC on its side, inserted it where it belonged. "And this, is where the phone jack goes." He was pointing to the PC, and we both looked at each other at the same time.

"There's no phone!" We said together. Shit, I knew there was something missing. I reached up to turn on the overhead lamp. I couldn't find a chain or switch. "fuck, what now?" I mumbled. I looked up into the lamp, and quietly got Peppers attention. "Hey, bro, how many wires does a light need to work?" I asked.

"Two Chief. Jeez, you do suck at electronics, don't you."

"Do not crack wise, Meatwhistle. It was 'spose to be a rhetorical question." I pointed up into the lamp. "Check it out. We have some more uninvited company."

I waited patiently while Pepper did his survey of our insect, and he let out a low, long whistle as he shook his head.

"Whatsa' matter?"

"This is a little more high tech."

I raised an eyebrow in response to his comment. "Do tell."

"Fiber Optics, bro."

"You mean as in the Dime Lady?" OK, so I've already admitted to being a son of a bitch. Being a smart ass was not out of the question.

"Cute wise ass, yeah, somethin' like that." He picked up my Zippo from the table, opened it, then struck a flame. Lighting it up,

77

he held it to one of the optics. There was a slight pop and the smell of burning fiberglass. "Cha ching! Man, they aren't goin' to be happy about this at all. Oh well, joke 'em if they can't take a fuck! OK, let's solve your modem problem." I just watched him, ready to be awed. This was one area he did not need help in. Next to Ponce, he was one of the most proficient electronic wiz's I had ever known.

He grabbed a chair, and set it under the smoke detector. Then, reaching for his Leatherman tool, he took it out of its sheath, and handed it to me. Next he found his screwdriver with its various bits and handed them to me as well. He climbed up on the chair and asked for the screwdriver with a the Philips bit. "Now, let's see just how high tech this place really is........."

Slowly he removed the cover to the detector, and peered into its wires and workings. "Bingo! Hey Row, in that opened bag on my bed is a roll of telephone wire, if you would be so kind?"

I rummaged through it, finding all kinds of odd shit in his bag. Finally I found it. "Here!"

"Thanks. Now, this here is a straight line to the phone box for the Fire Department. Obviously a seldom used line. I was standing, looking up into that detector with my mouth open as he did his thing. He looked down at me. "You payin' attention?" He asked, "there's gonna be a test on this shit later."

"Bite me, I'm with ya."

"OK, now the phone line is basically a secure line with only one jack. Most likely near the alarm box. Now, the trick is, to tap into it without cuttin' through it. Otherwise it will send a signal to the monitor and will throw an alert that someone is tryin' to disarm it." He used his Emerson Folding Knife and trimmed away the insulation. He continued, "the other thing ya gotta be careful of, is touchin' the wires together. That'll ground out the system, makin' it think there's a fire."

I unspooled about twenty feet of wire that Pepper needed, and stripped the insulation off of it. I handed it to him and he twisted the wires together. "Row, get some of that electrical tape will ya? It's in the bag too." He taped the connections and then wrapped the wire around the sprinkler pipe that ran in the ceiling to keep it from pulling apart. He dropped down from the chair and went to his bag. I swear it was like watching someone in a circus. It was amazing what he could pull out of his bag. Even more so, because he knew what to do with all that shit. He pulled out a module phone jack end and a pair of telephone repair pliers made of heavy-duty nonconductive plastic. According to him, you could get the whole kit at your local Radio Shack, along with the how-to on setting up your own phone lines. Gee, and I thought all he did was chase pussy.

I sat down by my lap top and waited for Pepper's thumbs up. Once given, I turned on the switch. It ran through its startup of systems, and I couldn't have been happier. Then all of a sudden, my eyes about fall out of their sockets. Janet had gotten a pic made of herself and she was on my monitor with nothing more than pasties and a G-string! Pepper was howling with laughter and I knew it was something I was never gonna live down. The pic was animated and she would bend over, blow a kiss then stand tall again. She had managed to have her face superimposed over the models.

"Hey Row, have I seen her in some club before?"

"Fuck you." Yep, he was not going to let me forget that one. I noticed a small square with a click here for more. I guided the mouse, clicked, and it was Pepper's turn. Likewise there was a pic of Sharon, and all of her glory, also superimposed. He had gone back to his sweep, and I was going to enjoy giving him shit immensely. "Um Pepper, there is something here you might want to see."

He walked over to where I sat and looked over my shoulder. "Holy Shit!! He rasped, as he stopped to look at her. We watched her animation, and from what we saw, he was slightly tweaked, and I was laughing my ass off. She had also gone into the same pose as Janet. Standing tall, then bending over seductively. Except, instead of a kiss, she brought her hand up and flipped him off. It made my fuckin' day to see the look on his face.

"Fuck. You. Rowdy."

Still laughing, I went back to my computer. I got rid of the skin flicks, and inserted the phone jack into its proper slot and dialed up the server. The modem card was excellent. It was 56K, which was even faster then the one I had at home. Slicker-n-snot and faster than hell on wheels. This would be great for uploading and downloading our shit. I logged onto my E-mail provider and checked for messages. I had two from Janet and one again from my joke pal. I read and replied to each, and sent a message to "Mom", to let her know her boys were well and good. I read the few jokes to Pepper, and had him in a better mood. "Hey, have you figured it out yet? If it's a he or she?"

"Negative. It won't tell me, I can't tell, and I haven't asked.

"Hmmm, maybe one of these days IT will 'fess up. Better yet, we have those high friends in low places that could find out for you, if you really want to know."

I looked back at him and just shook my head. "Dammit Pep, not all of the world wants to be treated as if they were part of an Op. I wouldn't dream of invading "its" privacy. He or she has obvious reasons for not letting me know. I would only do so if it were imperative to know. Got it? Do not take this as a challenge that you need to fulfill. Leave it up to me bro."

"Damn Row, I was jokin'. I think someone needs to get laid, and badly."

"Sorry, man."

After I finished playing around on-line, Pepper spooled up the phone line. Stuffing it behind the cover of the detector, he screwed it back into place. We finished stowing away the rest of our gear and I began to thumb through the manual. It was broken down into a listing of categories: Physical training, mental conditioning, shooting drills; which included a crash course in sniping, close quarter combat/CBQ knife fighting, chemical agents, first aid, basic demolition/improvised explosive device (IED), recognition and driver training. All of this and who knew what else as a cherry on top.

"Did you notice the Budweiser on Red Dog's breast? He my dear brother, is a SEAL Team Commander."

"If you remember ass bite, I got a fun-filled up close and personal with him. I saw the hair in his nose."

"Yeah, you did."

He laughed about that one and was still laughing as he walked into the bathroom. I headed outside for a smoke. I just needed some time to think about everything. Man, what I just read in that manual was what I had always wanted to learn, but the intensity of the place, I didn't expect. That was putting me at a disadvantage, which I would have to quickly remedy.

I stepped through the doors and breathed in the cool desert air. Fortunately for us, we were at the end of the hall and our outside terrace faced away from everyone and afforded us some privacy. Or so I thought. I heard that familiar whirring sound of nylon against metal and looked up. There was Bina doing her repelling and rope climbing practice, and she was headed for our veranda from her room above us.

"Uh, nice evening for a climb." I commented.

Her cheeks were rosy red from the chilled air and workout. "Yes, I love it."

Looking in our room, Bina released the clips on her harness and laid it gently on the terrace. Pepper came out of the bathroom and stopped dead in his tracks, wearing only his Calvin's. He was surprised to find a woman in the room, especially since she would have had to walk by him to get into the room. He crossed his arms across his chest. "The thing about it is, I don't remember ordering a woman," he said with a smirk.

Bina smiled at Pepper and winked as she put a finger to her lips to shush him. "No need to whisper here, we had the room fumigated," Pepper replied.

"I see. You boys are quite talented."

"So, what can we do for you tonight?" I asked, as I motioned to the table and chairs with my head. The three of us sat down.

"How do you know David?" She asked me.

Pepper looked at us both intently. He was wondering the same thing. Well, I don't share everything with the little shit.

Aaron Ben David Solomon, is a six foot, medium built Israeli, who I just call David. We had met at a Bar Mitzvah for a mutual friend. We were to provide the protection for that event, but as things turned out, it was more of a babysitting job then anything else. By the end of the evening, we were reduced to valets, opening and closing doors for the guests. Aaron and I stroked and joked most of the evening talking about ourselves. Both of us trying to out do the other. David had spent ten years in the Israeli Army with the last four in the Mossad, Special Services Division. After our meeting, we kept in touch.

If he were in town, we would get together for dinner, drinks or go shooting if time permitted. When my schedule allowed it, I would pick up David and his principal at the airport, in a rented luxury car and drive them around. It usually paid quite well, and he and I would exchange ideas, information, and copious amounts of Tequila. During one of our many conversations, he told me about his older sister, whose footsteps he was following in.

In Israel's military, the men and women were treated the same. It was quite possible for a female officer to command a special forces unit full of men, and be respected and obeyed to the letter. David told me his sister was one of Israel's top officer's and a great warrior. He had shared many stories of her, and I knew he admired and loved her very much.

Bina had ten years on her baby brother, but the one thing she had that he didn't was patience. Bina bided her time in the service and slowly rose in rank before retiring. David on the other hand, ramrodded his way through the system, charging up the ranks. So, at the ripe old age of 33, he sat behind a desk pushing paper instead of doing field Ops. Whether he was willing to admit or not, he had shot himself in the foot and had to live with it.

Bina had made the connection of who I was when I had my spiritual encounter with Red Dog in the mess. She picked up on the name, and remembered it from one of David's stories. She figured she would play a prank on me. Ha ha, fuck me running. I would be the Dog's personal whipping boy for the next six weeks because of it. During our impromptu pow-wow, Bina explained why she was with us.

It seemed there was a president of a corporation we would be working with. He had a wife and two children. Now, that's not unusual in itself. However, Mrs. P.O.T.C. (President of the Corporation) liked to maintain a high profile. With her high profile credit cards, in her high profile Niemen Marcus type stores, with her high profile cars and hobnobbing with her high profile friends, doing high profile lunches in high profile restaurants. Whew, high profile, getting my feelings on the situation? That was not the kind of principal one wanted on a gig.

Bina stood and stretched. "I think it is time for bed."

She walked to the veranda, and I helped her to put on her gear. Pepper and I told her she was always welcome and to drop down any time.

I smiled a big smile at her as she got ready to shimmy back up to her room. "By the way, we aren't very modest around here."

"Not to worry Calhoun's, if I see anything I do not recognize, I shall shoot it," she added with a crafty smile.

Pepper was laughing nervous-like, and I couldn't resist the jab. "You aren't a virgin are ya?" I asked her.

She winked at us, and as she swung out over the fencing of our balcony, she called out, "Shalom!"

"Dude! She is a fox!"

"Pepper! Put it back into your shorts!"
"I know....I know! Pepper, don't fuck the dancin' girls. Pepper, don't fuck the girl that does the laundry. Pepper, don't fuck the new girl on the team.

"Hey! I never said you couldn't fuck the dancing girl.

Pepper was laughing at me. "Damn, didn't think you'd catch that one," he said sheepishly.

"Aaaaaarg, lights out! G'nite dick head."

CHAPTER 14
NEW FRIENDS

After a rigorous morning of P.T., we were all herded into the mess hall for a general announcement. I dared to take a quick look at Red Dog, who was standing behind a makeshift podium. I noticed he was wearing his dress whites, when Pepper asked me, "Other than the movies, have you ever seen so much salad before?

(Now, for those of you following along, you're probably thinking the same thing I was, Salad? OK, so I bit too.) "Pepper, what the hell are you talking about?" I asked.

"Oh, my bad. Sorry bro, forgot you're civilian. Salad is what we call those ribbons and medals on his chest."

"Uh huh, thanks for that, and may I be the first to remind you, that nobody likes a smart ass."

Chuckling all the way to his seat, he saw the humor in the situation, and blew me a kiss then mouthed, "I love you man."

For a little hint, the Dog cleared his throat to let us know it was time to settle down so he could speak. It sure beat his usual style of S2, "Sit the fuck down, and shut the fuck up!" In an instant, the room was silent. "My name is Chief Warrant Officer, Roger Thomas."

He stopped briefly, as he looked about the room. I swear those Dog eyes always knew how to find me, no matter where I was. "I want all of us to be on a first name basis during your training. You, may call Chief. From this point on, you will salute me. From this point on, when I enter a room, you will stand at attention. Do I make myself clear!?

"Sir! Yes Sir! The room boomed in unison, answering his question.

"Excellent!" He countered.

The Chief eased himself out from behind his podium, and began to move about the room. He was inspecting each and every one of us, stopping momentarily to give that elevator look. First, he would look into your eyes, then slowly travel down to your feet, and back to your eyes again. There were several members whom he would shake his head in disgust, as he walked away. As he began to make his way toward Pepper and me, I was beginning to feel like Pavlov's dog. My automatic response, was a bad feeling in my stomach, every time he approached us. Those feelings were usually accompanied by the possibility that something terrible was about to happen. Shit, sometimes it just doesn't pay to be right. I held my breath as the Chief stopped in front of me, and was surprised by his appointing me the somewhat dubious honor, of Team Leader.

My initial thought was, "How bad could this be?" It wouldn't be until much later that I would find out exactly what that would entail. I would be responsible for: carrying the flag during our running exercises, making sure no one fell out of rank, calling the cadence, and finally, the most prestigious honor of all, or so I thought, was yelling at the top of my lungs, "Officer on deck!" whenever Chief Red Dog made an appearance. (There were more times than I care to count, that the son of a bitch would sneak up on me and I was unable to shout out. The punishment for that was vile).

After my anointment, the Chief began to walk away. Pepper rolled his eyes and whispered, "teachers pet."

The Chief spun on his heels like a child's top and shouted, "I heard that!" Pepper then bit his lip as if to try to take it back. "I saw that!" Chief bellowed. I swallowed hard, hoping he hadn't heard that.

Chief took his place back at the podium. He pointed to a tall, thin, black guy, standing in the front. "You! Come here! I need a volunteer!" The man took two steps and was immediately standing by the Chief's side.

Chief had asked him if he had any military service, to which the cadet barked, "Sir, United States Army, 82nd Airborne, Sir!"

"Very good son."

This cadet we affectionately named Axel (from the character on Beverly Hills Cop), stood smartly at attention. The Chief motioned for us all to move closer, so that we might gaze upon the prodigal son. He pointed out the correct way to stand at attention, insisting he would not tolerate any other way. Next he had Axel stand at parade rest, again showing the proper stance. Our attention next, was focused onto Axel's feet, so that we would learn the proper way to do an about-face. Now, I had already learned all these fancy dance steps in the Police Academy, but there was never much emphasis on it. I could see that Chief Red Dog was not the type to accept anything less than perfect. Perfect, therefore, would be what I would strive for.

Next came the salute. There was a certain way to salute a superior officer. He saw to it, we learned it. Red Dog made it abundantly clear, that not all officers were superior, but did however, deserve to be saluted. So, for the next hour, I got to practice yelling, "Officer on Deck!" Along with saluting, standing at attention, about-facing and parade-resting. Welcome to hell. "Hooyah Chief!" I said to myself.

We were allowed a break, where we gathered around the cans for a quick smoke. Bina, Pepper and me lit up, but didn't say a single word between us. Each of us focused in our own thoughts. If you had asked me what was going on in my head, I wouldn't have been able to say. But now, I can without question, tell you that I was wondering what the fuck was I doing there. I sure as shit knew I could do all that was required of me, and then some. Yet, something kept telling me, I was not in the right place at the right time.

I caught a glimpse of Chief Red Dog, quickly stood at attention and boomed, "Officer on Deck!" Almost undetectable, I swore I saw him nod, as if to say, "you got this one boy, but I'll getcha later." Which of course, he did.

"All right you candy-asses, put out the butts, and get back inside!" Barked Dog.

We quickly marched back into the mess, where the next several hours were spent with Chief covering chain of command and unit integrity. He explained to us in great detail the facts of life: Special Warfare hereafter, would be referred to as Spec War, and is waged upon your enemy in an unconventional manner.

The group that surrounds you is now your family.

At some point in time, you will ask one of your fellow cadets to put his life in your hands, or vice versa. If this team has no integrity, someone will die. It is entirely possible that more than one of you will die.

"During the next six weeks, I will push you all to the very limits of your body. I will give no thought to your race, creed, gender or age! I will treat you all the same. Just like shit! I want you all to pair up with your roommate. I want you to take that person by the hand, look into his eyes and repeat after me-- 'You are the most important thing in my life. Without you I am nothing. I will tuck you in at night, and I will wake you in the morning. We will eat, sleep, shit and fuck side by side. There is no greater importance than you. Together we will train, sweat, bleed and wage war. I am responsible for you. I must answer to you. For without you, I am nothing'." You have no idea, how hard this was to do with Pepper. I felt like such a dick, standing there holding his hand, but after saying this litany a few times, you begin to feel something inside. Something that can't be explained, but it's bigger than yourself. And your whole intent, is indeed to see to the well-being of this other individual.

Pepper and I were now considered partners for life. Pepper was now the only family I had. The Chief explained, that if they wanted us to have families, they would have been issued to us when we checked in. With that, Red turned to me and asked me to dismiss the men. I saluted the Chief, spun on my heels, and shouted out, "Dismissed!

With the dismissal ordered, I turned to leave. Only I didn't get very far. I was summoned by the Chief, "Calhoun, you and your brother are to report to my quarters at 1300hrs."

"Sir, yes sir"! I said, saluting. "Shit, now what?" I thought to myself. I found Pepper outside and informed him of our rendezvous with the Chief. We went back to our room and checked for bugs. We then double-checked and when we were sure there were none, we checked one more time.

"I got nothin'. Pepper went on to say, "if they are listenin', they're doin' it through the door with a glass to their ear". Pepper was right, there was nothing there. So, maybe I was being paranoid. OK, I was being paranoid, but that never got anyone killed.

At precisely 1259 hours, I took a deep breath and knocked on the Chief's door. "You're early!" He growled.

Pepper leaned forward and whispered, "lecture time".

I gulped hard and entered. The Chief was sitting with his back to us, at a modest wooden desk. He waved us over, and we stood at attention waiting for him to stop scribbling in his note pad. I took a look around the room, and what my eyes rested on, did not make me feel at ease. Two men in suits, sat in metal folding chairs near the sliding door to the veranda. One sat smoking a pipe, appearing to be in his late fifties looking tired, as he sat somewhat slumped in his chair. The other man looked to be in his late thirties, with an, I'm rarin' to go look on his face. He sat upright in his chair fidgeting. Each man had a large manila envelope.

"At ease gentlemen," the older of the two men said.

We stood at attention, waiting for the Chief to give us that order. "At ease men," the Chief said quietly with a smile. In one fluid motion, Pepper and I moved to parade rest. The Chief nodded at us.

"Which one of you gave us six years?" The younger suit asked.

"Sir, I did sir." Pepper replied. He didn't look so good all of the sudden.

"Son you did such a good job for the Navy, we want you back". I could hear the sarcasm, but I had no idea where this was going.

"Permission to speak freely sir?" Pepper asked.

"Granted," said the younger man. Unfortunately for him, he was the closest to Pepper. He hardly finished getting the word out of his mouth, before Pepper had his both hands around his throat and was on top of him like a pack of dogs on a three legged cat.

"Sonofabitch!" Yelled Chief, as he moved toward him.

Instinctively I moved toward the Chief. "On your six Pep!" I shouted.

I blind-sided the Chief with my forearm and spun, catching the older suit in the throat, just under his Adam's apple. He coughed and started choking as he hit his knees. I felt him come up on me, but it was too late. The Chief was moving too fast and landed a one-two combination. The first, hitting me in the kidney. The second, in my lower rib cage. I saw stars and hit the floor.

"Pepper," I gasped. Pepper was bent over the younger suit, still holding him by his neck and beating his head against the wall. He looked at me and leaned, thrusting his leg at the Chief and catching him dead center in the chest, lifting him up off the ground and throwing him back about five feet. I was struggling to stand upright, when I was deafened by a gunshot fired in close proximity.

"That will be quite enough," the older man rasped, as he stood where I had dropped him. A blood trail ran down his forehead, and he was holding a 9 mm Glock in his right hand. The smoke was still seeping from the barrel. "Enough of this fuckin' around!" He said, "I've got better things to do today than have the shit kicked out me". He definitely seemed moderately pissed. "Chief I would appreciate it if you would get control of your men." He added.

The younger man was having a hard time getting to his feet, no doubt from the lack of oxygen to his brain. His face was still a Barney shade of purple as he sputtered at Pepper, "you'll p...p...pay f..f...for that you f...f...fuck." Pepper flinched at him, and the guy jumped back.

I was finally regaining my composure, although my ribs had not. "You guys want to let us in on what the problem is? I asked, holding a hand to my ribs. "Seems pretty clear to me he doesn't want any part of reenlisting or does he need to illustrate that again?"

There was a knock at the door, and Chief shouted, "Everything is fine!" The room got very quiet.

The older man holstered his weapon, picked up folding chair, unfolded it and sat back down. To Pepper he said, "It's really quite simple actually. We have a weather station in the Arctic and it has your name on it, or you can choose what's behind door number two."

Pepper looked uneasy. "You gonna tell me, that out of the entire U.S. Navy, there's not one person who can run this weather station?"

"Not at all, Boatswains Mate Calhoun," the pipe man continued, "but currently, there is only one person here, who I want working for me on the assignment you are training for."

"You already have someone from the Navy," Pepper said, gesturing to the Chief.

"Its not Navy personnel I am after." He answered.

The old man sat back, looking directly at me. He looked like the cat that just ate the canary. It was at about that point where you could've knocked me over with a feather. "What could the Navy possibly want with me?" I asked the suits, "Wait a minute, it's all becoming very clear now. Your gonna use my brother as a bargaining chip, to get me to do something for you." My mind was moving at warp speed. "WTF,why me?" I thought to myself.

The older man interrupted my thoughts. "Mr. Calhoun you are a civilian, we use civilians from time to time when we feel that a government employee might be compromised while under cover."

I was beginning to put it all together. "This ain't just a quickie trainin' program and we're not here because we need to be trained are we?" I dared to ask, I hoped I was moving in the right direction. Judging by the beads of sweat forming on the younger mans upper lip, I was on to something.

"Mr. Calhoun, what I am about to tell you is a matter of national security." He said.

"Shit, this ought to be good." What else could I think to myself by this time?

The older man reached into his suit jacket pocket, pulled out a small bag of Borkum Riff and packed his pipe. He lit it, drew deeply and continued, "Two weeks ago you received a page from Richard Allbright, he informed you of a job in Mexico, yes?" I nodded. "How well do you know Allbright?" He asked.

"I know he was a sniper in the Army during the Viet Nam war. I know he worked for the company during that time and I know he makes terrible coffee."

He chortled. "Allbright recommended you for this assignment because he thinks you are the right man for the job. He also thinks you need to learn self control and that is why you are here."

"I see, and Pepper? He has the military way of thinking already." I just couldn't quite hit the nail on the head here with where this was all going.

The younger man entered the conversation. "We need someone

to assist us with the protection of the company in Mexico." He opened his envelope and spilled the contents onto his lap. "We have reason to believe that some of our technology is walking out the back door of this facility."

I couldn't resist. "What technology would that be?"

"The factory in Mexico manufactures computer chips that we use in our satellites and computers. These chips correspond with each other, so that tracking is made simple."

Now I don't consider myself an expert in computers, but I do know that if everyone had these chips, that would make tracking our satellites and their capabilities a very easy thing to do. OK, it was time to stop playing games. "Let me guess, you want me to infiltrate the warehouse and find out what's going on?" I asked, as I looked at both men. Neither of them wanted to look me in the eyes. I looked at Pepper. He was turning green just thinking about the arctic. I kept quiet for a minute, then looked at the Chief. He looked directly at me and gave a gentle nod as if to say, "Go ahead boy, speak your piece."

I broke my silence, "what's in it for me?"

The older man tapped the contents of his pipe on the floor, repacked it and said, "You will be able to sleep easy at night knowing your brother isn't freezing his balls off."

"I see," I said, as I reached into my pocket for my cigarettes. I pulled out two, lit both and handed one to Pep. I inhaled deeply and blew the smoke at the two suits. "I'll do it." I said quietly. Pepper seemed to be able to breath again, yet I could see the pain in his eyes for my being involved in this manipulation. He knew we didn't have a choice.

The older man opened his envelope and scattered its contents on the desk, "I have some papers for both of you to sign, then we will be on our way."

Fuck me running. TWICE.

CHAPTER 15
NEW LIFE

I had finally put my J.H.(John Hancock) on the last official document that would legally keep my ass bound to the Navy. How many did I sign? Too many to count, but each was more official looking than the one before it, and each bearing a seal that I didn't recognize. I held up the Mont Blanc pen for a moment, just looking at it, then deftly dropped it into my pocket. To the older man I said, "consider it my gift for services rendered." Catching Chief's eye, I just shook my head at the absurdity of our situation. Along with that, I was trying to ready myself for this new part of my life. I didn't have to like it, I just had to do it.

The next several weeks were spent finishing our training program. Everything that was in the training manual was covered extensively, not glossed over, but covered. Just when you thought you were getting it right, it was time to do it again. Let us not forget the immortal words of the great NFL coach Vince Lombardi, "Practice does not make perfect, only perfect practice makes perfect."

After completing all the sections of the training manual, and having check marks next to each, I felt confident. Think back to the first time you completed something on your own, that everyone said you could never do. Remember what that was like? You felt confidence. Confidence in yourself, confidence about yourself. That feeling would serve me well, throughout my career.

The feelings I had at our private graduation ceremony, were almost indescribable. The modified SPEC-WAR training I finished with my brothers-in-arms, had me more proud of myself than anything I had done before. Thomas Edison once said, "If we did all the things we are capable doing, we would literally astound ourselves." Well folks, I gotta be honest, I was astounded. I was the only one in attendance of this training that had no prior military experience, yet held my own with the best of the best.

During the post-grad ceremony, we were all given our assignments and rank. After everyone was given their diplomas, and rank assigned, I waited to hear what it was that I was to be doing. I figured nothing, because I was, in Allbright's words, "A no service mother-fucker." I would have no rank, thus have no responsibility. That would leave me free to keep up my end of the bargain with the company, and keep Pepper's ass out of the ice. Simply put, that was fuckin' A-OK by me.

I was ordered to dismiss the men, which I did with efficiency and perfection. After dismissal, I was shootin' the shit with Pepper and Bina, when I heard a page for me over the PA system. I was to report to Chief Warrant Officer Roger Thomas immediately. I double timed it over to the housing area and humped it up the stairs to the Chief's office. I knocked and entered.

The Chief was finishing up a phone call, and motioned me to sit in the chair facing him at his desk. I looked around the room and everything was packed. There were cardboard filing containers, several duffel bags and two suitcases on the bed. The Chief was already in civilian clothes: a pair of faded Levi's and a T-shirt that read "There is no problem that cannot be solved with the proper amount of high explosives." I grinned. The Chief replaced the phone in its cradle and looked back at me with a tired smile.

"Sir, you wanted to see me sir?"

"Yeah Rowdy, I did, and cut the sir shit. Call me by my first name, Chief" We chuckled lightly at his joke. "Listen Rowdy, the reason we didn't see fit to give you your rank out at the ceremony, is because it's nobody's business about your little secret."

He slid a manila envelope at me across the desk, as someone rapped on the door, "Come!" Chief called out. Hugo entered with two other men and began moving everything onto a cart in the hall, they were gone as quickly as they came. I opened the envelope and stared at the contents. The first thing to jump off the page at me, was the wax seal at the bottom of the first page. I looked at the top of the page and read it to myself. The Navy, in its infinite wisdom, had appointed me Lt. Commander, complete with the power that goes with it. WTF? It had to be a dream, I knew it. There were a lot of hereto fore's and whereas and a bunch of other fifteen dollar words, but the gist of it all, was I was second in command under Allbright, seems like maybe someone else doesn't trust him either.

The Chief put his hand on my shoulder. "Good luck son, use your rank wisely, see you in Mexico."

I never heard him leave. I must have been sitting there with the stupidest expression on my face. Partly disgust, because of how I came to get this prestigious title, the other, pride. Because in the same token, I knew I had earned it. I looked up and Chief was gone.

By the time I got back to our room, Pepper was packing. "You got a delivery while you were with the Chief," he said, as he pointed to the locker. There, hanging inside, was a set of dress whites. Pepper went to the door, opened it, looked out, closed, then locked it. "You wanna tell me what the fuck is goin on?" He demanded, with a harsh whisper.

I showed the papers to him. "I spend six years in the Navy and you get a commission to Lt. Commander? This is too much," he said with disgust.

"Hey, I didn't ask for this, ass bite. I did this for you, remember?! I think we should make the best of it and move on." I didn't mean to sound so pissed, but I was doing it for him.

"Well," he said with a smile, I am not saluting you!" He started laughing, so I knew we were okay again. "By the way this note came with the uniform," Pepper said, still laughing, as he handed it to me.

The note, scribbled roughly by hand, said only, "You have E-mail." "What the fuck? How could anyone know we had internet access?" I wondered, and I was pissed. "Pepper, it would seem that our counter-surveillance, has been less than adequate, read this."

After he read the note, he wadded it up and threw it at the smoke alarm. He was takin' this as a personal insult against his talent.

97

"Son of a bitch Row, I did everythin' I could think of to keep someone from figurin' this shit out!"

"Don't get tweaked bro, it's no big deal, we are leavin' Attica today, remember? So, they had some higher priced toys than you did, just let it go."

"Yeah, right, I guess so," he replied sadly.

I could tell that it was going to linger with Pepper, like a really bad taste in his mouth. Personally I was getting used to that taste, and the Navy was gonna see to it, that it became a regular part of my diet.

We set up the PC and accessed my mail server. There was a note from BUPERS, (Bureau of Personnel, US Navy). The message was very simple, "Do as Allbright says, but let us know what you are doing." I saved the address before deleting the message. I sent a note to Janet, and Pepper sent one to Sharon. I answered an E to the infamous, non-gendered joke pal, then we closed it all down, packed it all up and removed any sign we had access to a phone during our visit. A lot of good that did us at that point. Pepper made sure he left a surprise for the next person to inspect the batteries for that alarm.

Pepper and I packed in silence, then changed into our dress whites. We brought our bags downstairs and tossed everything in my truck which had been thoughtfully parked in front of the housing area. Ponce was standing outside saying goodbye to everyone. He saw us and let out a low whistle, and a fine salute. We said our good-byes and told him we would meet him at the Radisson in National City in thirty-six hours.

Pepper and I headed for Coronado and our last face to face meeting with the suits. The guard at the gate saluted us and waved us through. "Is it always that easy to get on a Navy base?" I asked.

"Look at the uniform you're wearin' meatwhistle."

"C'mon Pep, you can rent these at costume stores." We pulled up to the building marked JAG and got out.

As Pepper walked around to the front of the truck, he smiled, and motioned me to him. "Here's why you got in so easy." He was pointing to the blue and white decal affixed to the front bumper denoting rank and Military branch.

"Jeez, these guys think of everything," I said, shaking my head in disbelief.

Pepper and I moved down the hall in unison, junior officers jumping out of the way and throwing salutes in our direction. "You're supposed ta salute 'em back," he whispered. He was giggling like a school girl and enjoying the hell out of the entire situation.

We entered the main office and announced ourselves to the girl at the desk. "Just a minute Commander, they are finishing a meeting and will be ready for you shortly. Would you like some coffee?"

"Please." I tried to answer back with as much authority as I could muster.

The girl brought us each a mug of steaming coffee and went back to her desk. I couldn't help but notice the legs that were walking away. Pepper mouthed something about leaving her alone, then our mimed conversation was interrupted when her phone rang.

"Commander, they're ready for you now," said Legs.

"Thank you." I said. As I walked toward the door, Pepper was hot on my heels.

I removed my cover as I entered the office. There were several men, all but two who were in uniform. The pipe smoker came over and shook my hand, the son of a bitch was actually smiling. The younger guy from the last meeting was standing in the corner, scowling. Pepper tossed him a look of pure disdain. There was only one other man in a white uniform, Pepper whispered, "Admiral I think, I've never seen one this close."

The other man was in a tan shirt and green pants. He had the Marine Corp emblem on both collars and about five bowls of salad on his chest. "This is Colonel Waylon Thomas," said the pipe smoker, as he introduced us.

"Pleasure sir," I told him with a nod.

"Hell boy, the pleasure is all mine, I can assure you." He said with southern enthusiasm, as he shook my hand. It was statements like that, that I found unnerving.

The pipe smoker was apparently heading this shindig, "Gentlemen," he began, "lets all take our seats, shall we?" He turned off the lights and turned on a small projector. A picture of the plant in Mexico was on the wall now, I recognized it from our last meeting. "This is the manufacturing plant for all of our computer chips. We have reason to believe that some of our intelligence is being smuggled out of the plant."

I stuck my hand in the air.

"Yes, Commander?"

"You have no way of knowing if you're are getting everything that is made, do you?"

The pipe smoker coughed into his hand. "I'm sorry I didn't get that."

Now it was my turn to put him on the spot. I repeated my question.

"No, we don't," he answered quietly.

He turned off the projector and opened the blinds. "You're job Commander, is to make sure the POTC is safe, and that no harm comes to him while he is under your charge. Your secondary responsibility is keep your eyes open and report back to us anything unusual."

I stood up and faced him. "You don't trust Richard Allbright do you?" I demanded.

"Allbright has worked for the company for twenty-eight years!" The man looked flustered, then continued. "We have a pager we want you to wear and a cell phone for you to keep with you at all times. Both are secure. Dismissed."

"I have some other questions...," I insisted.

"Dismissed Commander!" He turned and walked out of the room through another door.

The younger man opened a drawer in a small corner desk and produced the pager and cellphone. He handed me a 3x5 card. "These are the important numbers for you to know. Good luck." The sneer he gave Pepper and me didn't go unnoticed, just merely set aside to be remembered for another day.

The Colonel saluted me, I returned it and spun to leave. As I walked out, I placed my mug on the girls desk, swung the door to the hall open, and walked swiftly to the truck.

Pepper, who had kept his hole shut the entire time, looked at me as if reading my mind. "Lets get drunk," he said. I saluted him, and his idea. We hopped in the truck and sped through the main gate, then headed back toward San Diego.

CHAPTER 16
A MAN WALKS INTO A BAR

Pepper and I pulled up to the Radisson, on National City Boulevard, in a town we immediately affectionately named Nasty City. I went to check us in and get a luggage cart and by the time I came back outside, my loving brother informed me that there were two bars within walking distance of the hotel. I kissed him on the cheek and told him how much I loved him. I tipped a bellboy $20 bucks to get our things settled into our room. He politely threw a salute our way, then cheerfully went about his business, while we cheerfully went about ours.

The bar that sat next to the hotel looked too trendy as far as bars go. You know the kind, the ones where the people have more holes from piercings than a colander. Well, that place was out of the question, so Pepper and I hoofed it around the corner and went into a little hole-in-the-wall called The Irish Pub. It couldn't be seen from the main drag in town, which was just the way we liked it. The only patrons of this kind of place, would be the locals.

We took a table in the back, ordered a pitcher and a few shots of Tequila to get us calmed down. The waitress could barely keep up with our shooter orders, and sometime after the fourth round, she just brought over a bottle and sat with us. Hell, we were the only people in the place anyway, what else did she have to do?

The bartender's name was Nick. He was a burly gent who didn't say much and had a well-used smile. The barmaid's name was Donna. She was a cute, well-built, dirty blond, who happened to have the most beautiful steel blue eyes I had ever seen. As it turned out, Donna was between boyfriends and was looking for a good time. Being a newly frocked officer, and having always been a gentleman, I felt it was my responsibility to frock her. Hooyah!

We went back to the hotel, and after several hours of slap and tickle, she kissed me gently and bid me goodnight. She told me on her way out, to make sure we came by the bar in the evenings after work. I winked at her and watched her strut out of the bedroom. I heard her say goodnight to Pepper, who was outside in the large common area of our hotel suite, watching TV.

As I climbed out of bed, Pepper came bounding in like a St. Bernard and jumped on the bed, landing right next to me. "Well?" He asked, looking just like a kid who was waiting for the next answer to a geometry test. "Gawd damn, she sure is hot!"

"A gentleman never kisses and tells," I said with a smirk.

"Yeah right," he laughed, "So how was she? I gotta know!"

With a big smile, and barely able to contain my hi-pro glo, I said, "Okay, okay, calm down...she was unbelievable. She wants us to come to the bar after work.

"Rowdy you are a fuckin' dog, "Pepper said, as he rolled around making barking sounds.

I went to take a shower, and could hear him every once in a while barking and howling. I lathered myself up and made sure to get behind my ears, shampooed and rinsed. As I reached for the soap to wash my face I dropped the bar. It had barely stopped spinning around the tub when Pepper burst in laughing, "You called?" He asked, as I was bent over picking up the soap. I started to laugh so hard I had tears running down my face.

I toweled off and perused my choices for evening wear. T-shits and jeans, fatigues, or dress whites. "Wonderful," I thought to myself. I definitely needed help in the dress wear department. I had no intention on buying new clothes until after the 0600 morning meeting. Fuck it, jeans and a T-shirt would do just fine.

I asked Pepper if he had any ideas for dinner, and he suggested a steakhouse about five minutes from the hotel. I grinned devilishly at him and told him I was in the mood for more pink meat.

Pepper drove us to the Chopping Block, and after a fantastic dinner of prime rib and several cold bottles of a really smooth White Zinfandel, we decided to sit in the bar for a few cold ones. This was the prime location to ogle the waitresses.

(I'm going to let you in on a little secret. There's a story behind this particular establishment. Local folklore has it that the restaurant was a front for prostitution back in the 70's and early 80's. There was a hotel just outside the back door and the waitresses doubled as hookers during mealtime. The only part of that tradition kept alive today is that the servers are DDG - drop dead gorgeous for you limp dicks out there).

As we sat at the bar getting our share of alcoholic refreshments, the guy next to us got into it with his significant other. The squabble seemed to be about whether or not he was looking at the girls. However, they moved quickly past that, to a recent affair that she had just found out about, and threw it in his face. This had progressed to an out and out brawl. Now normally, Pepper and I don't need anyone's encouragement to help a damsel in distress, but I swear we were goaded into this little brouhaha.

We were just sitting there, minding our own GODDAMNED business, when the guy told us not to get involved. I don't know about you folks, but that sure as hell sounded like a challenge to me. I glanced at my brother, and it was obvious to me, we were reading from the same sheet of music. With that, I followed suit as Pepper pushed his chair out ever so slowly. It seemed to take forever for that annoying grinding of the chair against the hardwood floors to stop. It quickly drew the attention of everyone in the room.

As we both came to our full standing position, it was apparent from the look on the asshole's face, that he had made a grave mistake. He stepped back looking like a monkey working on a math problem. You could almost see the thoughts running through his brain. He seemed to be struggling with some mental overload, and I couldn't believe that his head actually cocked sideways, as if searching for some way out of his predicament.

Lucky for him, neither of us liked to exert much energy while we were full of great food and spirits. He yelled some comment to his woman friend and made his way past us, turning sideways as he went, giving ample room and slightly bowing his head.

We took our seats and resumed making merry. Something I'm sure the establishment appreciated. As the crowd thinned, we moved towards the end of the bar and discussed our options as they related to our new job, which, in case you were keeping track of, were not many.

"So what's the plan?" Pepper asked.

I drained the rest of my beer and put the mug down gently on the bar. I started to say something and caught myself in mid thought. "I don't have a clue Pepper. I have heard when you are in a weak position, appear strong. That is what we shall do. Today we know nothing, the advantage is not ours. Tomorrow we should know more and we will take it from there."

In complete silence, he nodded, and we both suddenly seemed to be feeling our booze and our situation.

We tipped the bartender generously, and hugged our waitress goodnight. As we spilled out of the restaurant, it hit me like a ton of bricks. The smell of urine and destitution coming from a nearby parking lot where the bums were congregated. Pepper looked at me as I was reeling from the smell. "Whatsamatter?" He asked, as I began to feel nauseous. "You okay?"

"I'm fine," I whispered. I caught my bearings and straightened up. The smell threw me back to that night with Chief Bennett. We both got real quiet and continued our walk back to the truck.

I thought about Chief on the ride back to the hotel. I wished I had his wisdom to guide me through what I thought might be the toughest job I would ever have to do. I hoped I could indeed use my rank wisely as Red Dog had suggested. Suddenly my eyes became very tired.

I fell asleep that night dreaming of Chief. He, proud to see me in what he referred to as the only military uniform worth wearing. I promised myself to visit his grave in uniform and pay him my respects. I also vowed to find the little scumbag gang banger who fired one too many bullets that night but that would have to wait.

CHAPTER 17
FUN AT THE MALL

As I opened my eyes that next morning, I jumped. I had slept so soundly, I had actually forgotten where I was. Quite a change from what I had been used to for six weeks, that's for sure. I had set the alarm so I could wake early, to phone Janet and tell her I survived the training. I couldn't tell her I had been drafted though, I didn't think she would understand, and besides that, I wasn't sure who else might be listening on open lines. I was positive the company had tapped my lines into the house, and reasonably sure the hotel lines were tapped as well. I figured they could probably decipher E-mail too. What I had to tell her could wait until the weekend when I got home.

We chatted about the usual bullshit stuff - kids, bills, neighbors, and friends wanting to know what happened to me. I told her everything was fine, and I would be home that coming weekend. She laughed when I told her I would give her all the gory details then. I got to speak to the kids for a few minutes; it was good to hear their voices. Janet filled me in on her work. I was proud to hear that she got a raise and promotion, and with a little luck, she would be an investigator by year's end.

Pepper was stirring in the common room, grousing about something or another, when someone knocked at the door. I grabbed my .45 Glock off the nightstand and covered Pepper as he went to answer it. "Who's there?" he asked, in a mock high-pitched female tone.

"Chief Thomas!" Shouted Red Dog. Pepper cracked the door, confirming his presence and let him in.

The Chief was wearing jeans and a polo shirt with the SEAL team 5 logo on it. He walked in and shut the door behind him. He looked directly at me with concern and said, "I just spoke with naval intelligence." He paused a long moment, then continued. "They have confirmed that the Mexicans know we are coming. Allbright is stressed about the entire situation."

I looked at Pepper then Roger. "Am I being delusional thinking that this info will be shared with the rest of the team?" I asked facetiously.

As I lit my first cigarette of the day; the Chief smiled and shook his head. "My job is to keep you informed and alive, you're job... Well, you know what your job is. Keep your fuckin' head down, pay attention and maybe we will all come out of this with our balls intact. Understood?"

I tossed him a one-finger offhanded salute as he left. I got dressed and went downstairs to the restaurant where everybody had gathered, and were engaging in animated conversation. "Hey Rowdy, Pepper, over here!" Waved Ponce. He motioned to us from across the dining room.

"Hey man, wassup?" I asked, as I slapped him on the back with my morning greeting. The waitress appeared and poured us each a cup of coffee. We were informed breakfast was a self-serve buffet and gestured toward the breakfast bar, which was overflowing with food.

Now, I never said it was good food, I just said it was food. The muffins were hard, the bananas were brown, the orange juice tasted like battery acid, and I'm pretty sure the milk was an ongoing science experiment. The coffee was doing a passable imitation, so I stuck to that.

Allbright stuck his head in the room, and caught my attention. He is the only man I know, who could physically spend hours in the desert sun, and not even turn a shade of pink. He looked his usual pale self as he stuck a bony finger in my direction and methodically curled it over and over, motioning for me to come to him. I excused myself and headed toward him. As I rounded the corner near the elevator he grabbed me by my shirt and pulled me in with him. First he pushed the door close button, next, the button for the 12th floor.

That was when he made a very big mistake.

"I have no idea what deal you struck," he began, "I have no idea what you might think about your so-called rank, I have no idea what you have been told, and frankly I don't give a shit, but son, let me tell you something that may come as a shock to you. If you think you are in charge of this OP, you are sadly mistaken."

I looked him right in the eye as he spoke at me. "You are not in charge, I am in charge, can you say that?" I began to ask a question but, he cut me off. "I asked you a question, you don't answer me with a question, you useless piece of shit, understand?" I nodded vaguely.

That was unsatisfactory and he said so. The elevator came to a stop on the 12th floor, and as the doors opened, he pushed me out. I started to back up and he moved in closely. As we cleared the alcove, the elevator doors closed, sealing off my only immediate escape route. As I searched for the stairwell, I could see we were not alone. I counted two goons on my right and one on the left joining Allbright. So maybe not that big of a mistake I thought.

The one closest to Allbright moved in and he got it first. I backhanded him across the face. Coming halfway through my swing, I felt someone hit me across the back of my legs, my left knee buckled and I went down. Allbright was laughing, he was actually enjoying this! He came in closer and kneeled. Fortunately for him, too far away for me to reach him. With a sneer he said, "I want you to remember who's in charge boy." I never heard the elevator doors open but I remember the look on Allbright's face, when the Chief and Ponce accompanied by Pepper, Phil and Axel filled the alcove.

"Is there a problem Richard?" Asked Red Dog, with a mischievous smile on his face.

"Nah, we was just horsin' around, idn't that right son?"

I climbed to my feet with the help of Axel and looked directly at Allbright. With the shittiest look I could muster, I replied, "yeah, just funnin' is all."

I leaned in a little closer and whispered, "this is far from over old man. I don't know what your fuckin problem is, but you called me remember?"

He sneered at me, "you don't deserve to wear a uniform you haven't earned, you no service asshole." I moved past him toward the elevator. I looked back and asked him if he planned on holding the meeting or if we should just guess at what's going to happen in Mexico.

He lit a Marlboro Red, sucked in, then blew the smoke out in my direction. The doors opened and I stepped in with my reinforcements. As the doors closed, I WTF'd the guys, not believing my luck in the timing of it all.

Pepper sized it all up for me, "Red Dog came in and wanted to know where you were. We told him Allbright had called you over to the elevators. He said you weren't there, and after calling the rooms, his and ours, we decided to check the floor the elevator stopped on. The Chief said you might run into trouble with Allbright. He seemed mighty pissed about your recent promotion to NAVSPECWARGRP, and the fact you have a rank to go with it."

Ponce, Axel and Phil, stood quietly during our conversation. Phil, a Navy SEAL Rescue Diver, was, I'm sure, very interested in how a civilian could go from zero to Lt. Commander in six weeks. "That's ok," I thought to myself, so was I. The doors opened to the lobby and we stepped out. We headed towards the USS Enterprise Meeting Room, in the South Wing of the hotel.

A Japanese man and a Mexican man were sitting at a large conference table, when we finally managed to show up. The Asian was a young looking bookish kid named Toshio, and the Mexican guy, whose name was Flaco, looked to be about thirty-five years old. He had a round face and was probably thirty pounds overweight for his medium-built frame. Flaco was sweating profusely like he had just swallowed a handful of chili peppers even though the room was a comfortable sixty-eight degrees. Toshio sat patiently, even though our group was twenty-five minutes late.

Let me digress here for just a moment. Japanese people are very prompt. Did I say very? What I meant was anally retentive prompt. They do not like it when you are late. Sorry, let me rephrase that, they despise chaos and disorder. They cannot tolerate tardiness, and above all else, will not allow for even the smallest margin of error.

Japan has adopted the principle of ZD, that is Zero Defects. Let me categorize that for you, in case you got lost along the way. Zero means, none, nada, zip, nothing, nein, the big goose egg. Still with me? Now, with that said, you can probably guess how Toshio perceived us as a team. Not good.

I don't remember who said it first, but you never get a second chance to make a first impression. I bowed deeply upon entering the room. I apologized profusely in Japanese, repeating it over and over while bowing each time. Toshio looked at me. I wore the shame of embarrassment well. He nodded. It was perceived and understood I had taken the blame for my leader. That went a long way in Toshio's book, and would certainly go a long way with the Company as well. My quick and decisive action, coupled with the fact I said it in Japanese, was the break I needed to get my foot in the door. The rest would be easy. Toshio had seen me shoulder the burden of Richard's faux pas, and I had proven myself honorable in the first fifteen minutes of the meeting. I was running about two weeks ahead of schedule. It was already taking my mind off my throbbing leg. I laughed to myself and thought, "Fuck you Allbright and the horse you rode in on."

The meeting was just a general, bullshit getting to know you and you getting to know us type of thing. What we could and couldn't do. That left, at least in my mind anyway, a lot of open ground. Oh well, better to beg forgiveness, then plead for permission. The meeting broke, so the majority of us headed out to select our new wardrobes. Thank God sport coats and slacks or pressed jeans would now be the nom de rigueur. Pepper and I decided on the local Wal-Mart, for the lowbrow GQ look. It took about two hundred fifty dollars to get a new wardrobe for work, along with black jeans, socks, Calvin Klein underwear and various sundries.

We stopped by the local gun store near the hotel to stock up on ammo, cleaning supplies, and other goodies. You can't look good and have a dirty gun, can you? By the time we got back to the hotel, it was getting to be chow time. Pepper and I decided on Chinese and headed toward San Diego. After filling up on Mu Shu Pork, Cantonese Chicken, Mongolian Beef and Broccoli, Shrimp with Lobster Sauce, with plenty of flied lice, we were stuffed.

My brother suggested a game of play the tourist at the Horton Plaza in Downtown San Diego. Sure, what the hell, I figured, I would play along. Now, for those of you who have never been to, or seen the Horton Plaza, it is a huge indoor/outdoor mall, with several floors, and all kinds of shops. Because of the location, the mall was mostly upscale, and the shops reeked of money. FAO Schwartz has a store there. Hell, even Barbie has her own store there for christsake! That bitch really does have everything.

We mulled around, working off dinner, when Pepper saw the perfect woman. Or at least in his estimation she was. "Look at that man, she's got them throw up legs!"

I cocked my head and looked at him quizzically, and asked, "huh?"

"You know," he went on to say, "the kind of legs you want to throw up over your shoulders and wear like a feedbag!"

I shook my head, the boy definitely had a hard-on that just wouldn't quit! I waved and said, "See ya." Then he was gone.

I continued my casual stroll around the locals, dodging kids and moms chasing kids, and that's when I saw it. My heart raced. My palms got sweaty. I was in love. I stood frozen. Right before my very eyes, a real ... live... cigar shop. The kind that roll them right in front of you! As I stood looking through the window of the moderately sized store, I might have been drooling, I don't remember, but that's when I caught him out of the corner of my eye. A dark skinned fellow in a blue Adidas running suit. Ordinarily that wouldn't have even raised a red flag in my mind, however, he was wearing mirrored sunglasses and imitation lizard cowboy boots. I went into the store and purchased a couple of mild cigars. The clerk said they would be smoother than the ass of a sixteen-year-old girl. He winked at me and told me they wouldn't get me into near as much trouble either. I smiled back, paid the man and left.

When I came out of the store, Adidas man was gone. I moved down the walkway, looking into more windows, pretending to be interested in what was behind the glass. I bent over to peer into the storefront of a music box company, admiring what, I couldn't tell you, but I saw him again. I straightened up, and began to stroll in the opposite direction.

The most important thing about being tailed, is not to let on that you know, hence, you still have the element of surprise. Now, in this type of scenario, it's easy to detect whether or not you're being tailed. Especially by doing everything that I was doing. Stopping every so often, looking in the windows, going into a store and coming out looking as though you are lost. It affords you the opportunity to look around. These are the tricks of the trade, but, if the person following you is good, you shouldn't have seen him or her in the first place.

However, this guy wasn't very good. But just to be one hundred percent sure, I led him around some more. I kept hoping I would bump into Pepper, no such luck. The first question you might be asking, as I was, is who is this person following me? The second, why? Does Pepper have a tail too? "Screw 'em for now," I thought to myself. He was on his own, my brother could take care of himself.

I played grab ass around the mall, then decided to take my guest into the parking garage. I knew if I was lucky, and fast enough, I could lose him there. I headed toward the Broadway store and saw the overhead sign that pointed the way to the garage. As I rounded the corner, I ran as fast as I could, entering the double doors to the garage. I soon realized how VSF'd I really was. My tail had anticipated my move, and had entered the parking area through a door previous to the one I had found. Fuck me running.

He had a large smile on his bandito mustached face, and an Arkansas toothpick in his left hand. An Arkansas toothpick, is an affectionate name for an eight inch, (at least) double-edged knife. He moved closer and I sidestepped him, producing my Emerson folding knife. While opening it up, I smiled back, he didn't quite look so confident anymore. I stepped in closer and assumed an offensive posture. He sidestepped me and said, "I'm here to send a message. You bodyguards better not come across the border tomorrow." He grinned as we continued our little dance.

"Or what shitstain?" I asked.

He lunged, but I was ready for it. He was able to nick me across the shoulder as I ducked, then I caught him full across the back of his neck as he went by, spraying blood everywhere. He turned and lunged again. I parried and caught him across his chest cutting him deep and wide. He nicked me across my free hand as he flailed away at me. (OK, let's stop here for a minute. I don't give a rusty fuck what you see on TV, and in the movies. Knife fighting is dangerous, and no matter how good you are, you will get hurt, even if it's a nick. There is no way to disarm or terminate your attacker without getting close, unless you have a gun. That option, unfortunately, was not available to me at that time.)

He was losing a lot of blood and was becoming desperate. My new friend, MIQ, that's Mexican In Question, was beginning to tire, and to top it all off, we seemed to be drawing a crowd. As he made his last feeble attempt to stick me, I dropped my knife, catching him off guard. Grabbing his arm, I trapped it between my side and arm, as I spun around opposite of the way he was facing, I snapped his elbow in half at the joint. He squealed, then dropped the knife.

I spun again, grabbing his bloody collar and sent him careening toward the edge of the second floor. He stumbled and as he was attempting to catch his balance, I drop kicked him in the chest tossing him off into space. He screamed for a second, and I heard what sounded like a hollow thud, somewhat akin to a watermelon being hit with a bat. I looked over the edge, and there, lying in the street, amid the screams of people entering and exiting the Broadway, was my MIQ.

I could hear clapping from below, and sure enough, there was Pepper giving me thumbs up and shaking his head. The crowd that had assembled was of fairly good size, and I swear I had all the good intentions in the world to make my escape at that point. However, Officers Murphy, Murphy and Murphy had already filed out of the elevator and surrounded me. The officers had formed a circle defense perimeter around yours truly. Nobody wanted to put his or her hands on me, until the HazMat Team showed up, seeing as how I was covered in blood and all. Pepper was standing in the midst of the crowd, not wanting to attract any undue attention, but wanting to hear what was going on.

The HazMat boys had me cleaned up in no time, then just when I thought the boys in blue were going to leave me alone, I was cuffed, stuffed, screwed, blued and tafuckintooed. The PIC, that's Person in Charge, had at least given me my cigarettes and lighter in the car. He had switched the cuffs to the front so I could sit and smoke while they investigated. I had only been in the backseat for about a half an hour, when two, dirtbagish-looking guys, came looking for the PIC. They argued for about five minutes, came over to the car, then let me out.

"Stand up," the guy with the beard said to me. The other one, the one with the ponytail unlocked my cuffs and walked me over to their car. As I surveyed the carnage and the crowd, I spied Pepper talking to one of the cops. He gave me a covert thumbs up as I passed.

I was working on my fifth cigarette, when the bearded one broke his silence. "So, I imagine you were just minding your own business, when Señor Knife Welding Maniac jumped you here in the parking structure?"

"Wow! I am amazed! I can't believe you figured it out all by yourselves," I said, facetiously. I was laying the sarcasm on pretty heavy. Both of them wheeled around at the same time and looked at me. "Did the late Ernesto Dominion have anything to say before you practiced your Thanksgiving skills on him?" Asked the guy with the greasy pony tail, his tone matching mine.

I nodded, and said, "Yeah, he said something about teaching me a lesson and using me as an example. Don't quote me on that, but that's about all I remember. Who are you guys anyway?" I asked, and stopped walking.

The two of them looked at each other a moment, and the bearded one shrugged as if to say, "What the fuck?" and answered, "We work for part of a drug interdiction task force. Every day, seven of us go to Mexico and seven Mexicans come across to the U.S. This helps us identify and arrest smugglers, mules and players."

"And what has this got to do with me?" I asked. I was starting to put it together before he could fill me in. What they told me only confirmed my suspicions. The Mexican Drug Cartel had gotten it into their heads, that we Americans were coming down there to interrupt the drug trade in our spare time. Señor Dominion was the son of only one side of the Cartel families operating down in Tijuana. They caught a whiff of us and figured the bodyguard gig was just a cover for DEA guys.

I listened as the pony tail guy, answered all my suspicions. Shit, there are some days where you just hate to be right. Fuckin' A, we hadn't even crossed the border yet, and we were already walking into an ambush, but nobody knew it but Pepper and me. Allbright would never believe what happened here, and even if he did, he would be too damn stubborn to do something about it. We were about to experience BOHICA (Bend Over Here It Comes Again).

After my interview, Pepper and I headed across the bridge to Coronado, and after getting poor directions from the MP at the gate (doesn't anybody know how to put an address on a building anymore)?, we arrived in front of an unassuming building where the Navy's Branch Intelligence Gathering Department was. After some bribery and threats of waking the Base CO to get what we wanted, the little geek in the office finally gave in.

"All we want is everything you have on Ernesto Dominion and

his family from the last six months. Thank you," I said curtly. I scribbled my E-mail address on a post-in note and gave it to him. "Forward everything you come up with. Goodnight."

"Yes, sir Commander." The little geek saluted, we did an immediate about face, and got the hell out of there.

I was up at 0500 checking my mail. There didn't seem to be a whole lot of information on the Dominion family, other than the usual drug trafficking, racketeering, prostitution and a string of bars in downtown Tijuana. What I was able to glean, is there was a war going on between the Cartel families along the California-Mexico border. Anyone perceived as a threat would be eliminated. Included with the Intel was a news clipping about a bodyguard who was followed across the border and killed near a small community called Rainbow, off the 15 Freeway, fifty miles north of the border.

Evidently, he was pulled over police style and executed. His attackers left a note on his chest warning other Americans working in Mexico, that this fate could befall them. The really unfortunate part of the entire situation though, was the fact that like a good law abiding citizen, his firearm was found in a lockbox, in the trunk, with the ammunition in another box, separate from the gun. Why was this you ask? How come a professionally trained bodyguard has his gun locked up and not on his person?

For those of you that don't reside in California, let me make a few points:

Point #1: You need a Concealed Weapons Carry Permit, to carry a gun concealed in California. Simple right?

Point #2: The permit process to apply, is tedious and discouraged by most Police Departments. You need a good reason for the permit.

Point #3: Body guarding is not considered a good reason. Why? Because that my friends, is how cops earn a second income. Departments have cut back so hard on our men and women in blue that they have turned to other ways of supplementing their income. Do I blame them? Not at all. Do I think it is shitty to shut out other hard working individuals from obtaining a permit so-that they may work and legally carry a gun? That answer is an emphatic yes!

Point #4: If one decided to go armed without a permit, he is subject to fine, imprisonment or both, including, but not limited to, losing his or her gun and all of this in the name of protecting oneself and their client.

I think it's bullshit, but until California gets off it's liberal ass and starts issuing permits to those who can pass a background check and a firearms safety and familiarization course, there are those out there who run the risk everyday of the four points listed above. Now I will climb down off my soapbox.

So basically, this poor bastard was fucked before he even knew what happened. So sorry Mrs. Bodyguard, your husband obeyed the rules and now he is dead, waxed by some shitball who is in this country illegally and carrying a concealed weapon, without, yup you guessed it, a permit.

However, I digress, the point I am trying to make, is we carry our guns everywhere we go, and for everything we do, well, umm...uh...except tonight. Everyone on the team would rather be tried by twelve than carried by six. End of Sermon.

I met with the Chief, and gave him a SITREP of everything we had found out. He shook his head and told me to inform Allbright, my team leader.

"Hooyah Chief," I said sarcastically.

Allbright was in no mood to hear any of it, of course, but attempt to him inform him, I did. According to his sources, who they were he wouldn't say, everything in Mexico was fine. The hostility toward the Americans had been solved by bribing a few high-ranking officials. As far as Richard was concerned, the team had free passage into and out of Mexico and we were going full steam ahead. I tried to suggest a bit of caution, but he wanted no part of it. "You have your orders Lieutenant, carry them out!" He barked full of sarcasm, ending any possible way out of this mess.

"Yes, Sir!" I countered. I said those words with remorse, and I said those words with hatred. I could see a blood bath coming and there was nothing I could do, but keep everyone on Defcon 5. The term FUBAR came quickly to mind.

As I keyed the mike to start our procession across the border at Otay Mesa into Tijuana, I had a bad feeling in the pit of my stomach, and told Ponce so.

"Must have been the coffee, Rowdy!" Ponce said with a chuckle.

God I hope so I thought to myself, I fuckin' hope so. I looked in the rearview mirror to see what the principal was doing. He didn't look half as nervous as I was. At the last minute, Richard decided to stay in Otay Mesa at the main plant. If we needed help he could call from there to Brown Field where we had a Helo waiting for emergency extraction purposes. Allbright had it all figured out. If we were all dick deep in Mexico and the shit hit the fan, no one could call for help.

"Gee Dick, why didn't I think of that?"

CHAPTER 18
FAMILY TIME

"How the hell am I supposed to be happy!? You're never home! And don't you even start in with me on how great the money is. What the hell difference does it make if you're never here?"

Fuck, like I've never heard this bullshit before, absolutely not the way I wanted spend a few days off while the Japanese were back in the land of the rising sun learning about new products that will be built at the Mexican plant.

I shifted my Stetson slightly, and take a deep draw off my Marl, and give her that beady, "This is really startin' to piss me off" look.

"Rowdy Calhoun, do not think for one minute that your bad ass look is gonna work with me! Don't you dare forget who knows you better than anyone else!"

Well, I do believe she's wrong about that one. One woman knew me better. Ruth, the one person who accepted me as I was, and listened to what I had to say, and to her, what I had to say was important.

"Janet, it isn't that I don't want to spend time with you. But God dammit, all I want to do after a long detail is to chill out! It's really hard to do that with you yellin' at me about one thing or another, or the kids runnin' around, and..."

"Rowdy, they're kids. It's what kids do! If you don't like it, maybe you should just..."

"Just what?"

"I don't know." Her voice is just barely over a whisper, and then the crying begins. I watch her as she runs from the kitchen to our bedroom, slammin then locking the door.

Fuck. I love my family. I really do. But I've only been home three days, after being gone for two months. I can't seem to make her understand that I need time to just be left alone. I need time to wash away that last detail; to feel comfortable again with the slightest noise, or odd shadow.

Meanwhile on the seedy side of town, Pepper watches the stripper as she slinks and slithers across the dance floor toward Pepper. He teases her with a sweet, crisp, twenty that he's dangling between two fingers, like a carrot baited for the rabbit. She is a slender redhead, and quickly saunters toward her tip. She leans over and her bare tits brush against his chest as she whispers, "I get off in fifteen minutes, meet me at the bar?" She then takes the offered twenty between her teeth from his waiting fingers.

With a wink and a nod from Pepper, she knows he will be waiting for her. She slowly stands upright, and turns her backside toward him. "Red" then bends over to pick up the twenty that "accidentally" fell to the floor. He gets a real, up-close look at her "ass"ets, then she again stand straight and tall.

Pepper can see that she is sliding her tip inside her G-string. She glances back one last time, spanks her tattooed ass, then she gracefully makes her way toward the dressing rooms. Pepper adjusts himself before standing to go to his waiting position at the bar. Anticipation is growing for what the evening holds, and it's also growing in front of his pants.

Pepper is now beyond the pleasantries of the how-do-you-do's and what's a nice girl like you doing in a place like this. No one could ever accuse him of being excessively romantic. As he admires the curves and valleys of "Red, he thinks to himself, 'Always did like a good lay in the back of my pickup." He gives his full attention to the two creamy white tits that find their way into his hands and mouth. As he rolls her erect nipple in one hand, he gently bites the other.

"Ooooh baby, I love to have my nipples bitten!" She moans with each tug he makes against her, and she pulls his head closer to her chest.

He can't help but notice the radiant beauty of this woman, and thinks to himself, "She's meant for better things then this place." But, it is a fleeting thought as he sucks in more of her tit into his mouth. He loves hearing her sighs and moans, and couldn't get enough.

I walk into the kitchen, grab the handle of the fridge and reach for an ice cold Dos Equis. The hiss of the escaping carbonation, makes the silence seem more deafening. Takin' a long drink, I'm enjoying the flavor as it goes down. "Aaahhh, man's best friend, and I'm not talking about a dog either. I walk to my bedroom in an attempt to assess Janet's mood. I can still hear her crying, so I tip toe by the door and head for the den. "Give her some time to herself." At least that's what I tell myself. Hey, it sounds like the right thing to do. I kick back in my favorite chair and reach for the remote control to see what's on the tube

I'm pretty much mind melding with the TV, and I'm brought back to reality with the shrill sound of the phone as it rings next to me. "I'll get it!" I half snarl and yell, to anyone who might be listening, as I reach for the phone. "This better be good," I answer.

There's a slight hesitation in the caller, and I hear, "Fuck you and your brother! Die bodyguard!"

"Shit! Janet get down!" I yell to her, as I run down the hall. I hit the door at full speed, splintering it as I burst into the room. As I barrel into our bedroom, I see a man holding a large knife to my wife's throat. Without hesitation, I dive for the piece of shit that dared to enter into MY private domain. I have the man by the throat, (my personal favorite in efficiency to dispatch a bad guy).

"Three things you don't fuck with dick wad: a man's gun, his wife and his hog. As I squeeze a little tighter, I continue. "And NOT necessarily in THAT order!! I tighten my grip for the last time, and pull away the flesh and muscle that are under my fingers, away from the mans neck. He actually has a startled look on his face.

I lean toward his face and press my nose against his. I stare deeply into his dying eyes and I could feel his last warm breath seeping from the gash in his neck. " There is no honor in stabbing a man in the back." But if you're going to take a man's life, look him in the eyes. I drop him like a rag doll and spin around toward Janet.

"Shit, Janet, are you OK? I'm sorry.

"Since when does work follow you home?"

I just look at her. Other than her hands shakin, she has no fear in her voice, and only sounds moderately pissed for the intrusion. "Well, hon, this is apparently an exception." Then I remember what the phone caller said, 'And your brother!'

"Oh shit!!" I jump across the bed and grab the phone.

Janet, is now visibly upset, because she sees the fear in my face. "What is it!?"

"Pepper! The caller said you AND your brother! I gotta warn him!"

"Do you know where he is?"

"I'll page him!" As I start to dial his number, I hear Pepper on the other line.

"Hey, hello! Hello!? Get the hell outta the house! I'll explain later!"

"Slow down Pepper, it's over. For now anyway. Whoever it is, sent someone to kill Janet and me. Are you okay?" We are both, way too charged up right now, and someone is gonna pay for this. And pay dearly.

"It'll take about ten bucks in quarters ta clean out the back of my pickup, otherwise I'm fine. Shit, probably need a new carpet kit too."

The obviously natural red head was lying in a shallow pool of her own blood in the back of Pepper's '95 Chevy C1500 4X4. To dispose of her body properly, would be a definite challenge without attracting undue attention. Pepper takes care of that "challenge," by dumping the would-be assassin into the police department's huge dumpster. A quick run to the coin operated car wash, has Pepper back in business and heading to my place.

"Ruth!" Shit, I had forgotten all about her.

"How can you bring her name up at a time like this, Rowdy!?"

"She's next!" I didn't know how I knew this, but it was a really bad feelin' I was gettin' about the whole fuckin' thing.

Janet tried, unsuccessfully, to get through, and out of frustration, threw the phone on the bed. "You call her, it just keeps ringing and ringing."

"I gotta go!" I rush to the closet, and reach into my hidden cache, to retrieve two Glocks, a 9 mm, my hand cannon and my .45 ACP. Slidin' the .45 into a SOB holster I grab the shoulder holster for the 9er. Reachin' into yet another hidey hole, I pull out two spare magz for both weapons. When it's all said and done, I am sportin' one hundred and four rounds.

"You lookin' to start a God damn war?"

I know Janet didn't know what was going on, and I didn't have time to explain it. "To stop one!"

"I'm goin' with you!" Before I could say yea or nae, she grabs the shoulder holster and the smaller of the two weapons. "I told you, you go no where near Costa Mesa without a chaperone. Especially since you are going to see HER!" She ran out of the room, leaving me with my mouth open, and feeling quite proud of her at the same time.

I grab my ankle length Australian duster and was stepping into it as I continue to make my way out of the house. I see Janet sitting in our lifted white Chevy Blazer, with a smug look of confidence as I near her. But that look doesn't last long, as I continue past the Blazer toward a blue plastic cover leaning against the side of the house. Knowing she is watching me, I fold back the tarp with patience that I had been trained in. I was standing in front of the object to be uncovered, and Janet didn't have a clue as to what was there. I step away to reveal the '91 Harley Davidson Fat Boy.

She told me this later, but Janet was thinking to herself, "It is beautiful." And as she watched my strong legs straddle the ebony bike, she thought, "Mmmm you have never looked so sexy." Well, again, it is strange what will go through someone's mind when adrenaline is flowin' and chaos is near.

I reach with a black gloved hand, and press my thumb to the starter button. The 80 cubic inch motor thundered to life, and the blue chrome drag pipes belched out flame, alternating from one pipe to the other. "Hmmm a little too rich." As Janet comes up to me, I hand her a leather covered skullcap. It was the smallest street legal helmet made and I had her name embossed in silver across the smooth black surface.

"Hey, Row, when did u finish it?" Gently she trails her fingertips over the letters spelling out her name.

"The last time I was home, I picked up the last couple of pieces I needed from the Harley dealer in Berdoo." I kicked up the chrome stand with my size thirteen Rockies, and Janet climbs on. The bike barely budged from her extra weight as she too straddled the high powered beauty on wheels. (Her not knowing the bike was finally assembled was just another example of how out-of-touch we were with each other)

I whack open the throttle, the thundering was so loud, that our neighbors musta thought that Thor himself was banging on their doors. With a squeal and wide black track mark, I head up the street. Shifting my feet to the highway bars, I settle into the custom Corbin seat after entering the 215 Freeway. Janet squeezes tightly around me telling me she loves me. I don't hear her......but I don't have to. I already know.

125

CHAPTER 19
CUT AND RUN

The 91 Freeway was fucked as usual, and it didn't help that a light mist had started to fall. I sure as shit was glad I had decided to add a windscreen to my prized creation. As I weaved in and out of the heavy traffic, I shouted to Janet, "This is why I took the bike!" With the truck, we could have been stuck for God knows how long, and time was of the essence. I had to get to Ruth. Thankfully, I made it to 55 South in record time.

Janet heard a buzzing and yelled, "What's that noise?"

"It's a cell phone!" I shouted back.

I answered the phone with a loud, gruff, "yeah!"

"I'd recognize your handy work anywhere!" Started Pepper, "Good work bro!"

I laughed and answered, "Ya liked that huh?"

"Where the hell are you Row?"

"I'm headed to Ruth's, she doesn't answer the phone!"

"Okay, I'm on my way, and will meetcha there!"

As I approached the turn-off to Ruth's street, I cut the motor and coasted to an alley that ran behind Ruth's house. "Stay here," I whispered to Janet.

I walked around to the front of the house, and checked out the carport. Putting my hand on the hood of Ruth's car, told me it was still warm, so I knew she hadn't been home long. "Why didn't her machine pick up," I wondered.

I quietly checked the front door, to find it unlocked. Someone had to be waiting for me. I headed back toward Janet, and when she could see me, I motioned for her to come to me. "Janet, The front door is unlocked, her car is here, and I hear absolutely nothing from the inside of the house. It's too damn quiet. I want you to go through the front door creating a disturbance. I don't know, perhaps just acting like a neighbor. You know, knock, then enter, talking as if you're used to making yourself at home." She rolled her eyes at me, but I didn't have time for her shit, so continued,

"I'm gonna go through the upstairs back window and work my way down."

I hugged her, and whispered, "when the shit hits the fan, hit the floor. Do not try to be a hero." I couldn't help but think how fortunate we were that our kids were at their grandmother's house that night.

"Rowdy, please be careful," she whispered back to me.

She disappeared around the corner, and I ran to the fence. Holding onto it and the gutter, I scaled the wall to the balcony two floors up, hoisted myself over it, then checked the sliding glass doors. Locked. "Fuck," I said to myself. I pulled out my Emerson, and pried the frame away from the clasp on the door. "Thank God for cheap American locks," I thought.

Carefully I slid open the door, just enough to crawl through it. A quick recon, told me I was alone in the room. To avoid any floor creaking, I moved slowly, with long strides, to make my way to the door. As I reached the door, I heard a loud crash of broken glass, that masked the sounds I might have made as I crossed the threshold to the stairway. I could see two figures. One appeared to be a man, the other a woman. It didn't appear to be Ruth, she had a smaller stature.

I made my way down the stairs, grabbing the man from behind. With my left hand, I reached for his neck, with the other hand, I tore at the Glock tucked inside his pants at the small of his back. The man made a swift recovery, and we began to struggle for the gun.

The guy was frustrating me, and beginning to piss me off.

I noticed the woman made her way to where Ruth and her kids were bound and gagged. I could do nothing, but deal with the asshole bent on attempting to take control of the Glock. I saw her make her way toward Ruth's youngest, then heard the shot go off. The woman dropped like a sack of shit, and Ruth looked as if she might gag, as the woman landed at her feet, with most of her face splattered against the wall behind her.

I couldn't worry about Ruth being able to hold down her dinner, I had problems of my own. This little fucker was more spry than I was. I had to find a way to make one solid punch, even if it meant getting seriously hurt in the process. He managed to knock the gun out of my hand and neither of us wanted to be the first to bend over to recover it, so around and around we went.

Our little game of thrust and parry with our fists began to wear thin on the intruder, as I could see he started to tire. His eyes had that desperate, trapped look. "That's when they really get dangerous," I thought to myself, "stay sharp Calhoun!"

The man produced a fairly large knife from the inside of his coat and lunged at me. A sidestep move I had learned in training at Diego prepared me for it, and it worked. As he shot past me, I grabbed his arm at the wrist, lifting it straight up. I backhanded his elbow and with my other hand, I broke it easily. With his knife still clutched in his hand, I guided it with the skill of a surgeon to his new home. His kidney.

I yanked up on the knife after it sank to the hilt and cut the man as far as his bent arm would let him. Reaching behind me, I took out my Emerson from its sheath, and sank it deep into the man's chest. As I removed it, all that could be heard was a sucking sound. Something like a boot, deep in mud as its owner pulls it out.

We could hear the roar of a familiar engine, Pepper was making his way to us, and you could hear it through the entire neighborhood. Janet looked at me with a chuckle, and said, "Nothing like making an entrance."

Pepper burst through the door with a Ruger semi-automatic in each hand. Once he realized everything was under control, he pouted and said, "Son-of-a-bitch, I always miss out on all the fun!

I was busy cutting the electrical cords off of Ruth and her three kids when Ruth finally seemed to come out of her shock. "How.....how did you know?" She cried.

We could hear the faint whine of sirens in the distance, "no time now to explain it Ruth, have you got a place to stay other than your mothers?"

"Nnnn....no, we don't." She answered, the terror in her eyes obvious to anyone who looked into them.

I glanced over at Janet. "You've got to be kidding me, right? Asked Pepper, "You can't go back to your place, the cops will be all over you house like stink on shit."

I realized he was right, and reached for my cell phone. I punched in the number and waited. "Waterfront Realty, may I help you?"

"Kim?" I asked, but not willing to say who I was.

"Rowdy? That you?" She answered.

"Hey, I need a favor."

"What else is new," she replied with sarcasm.

"I need a place to stash a few people for a few days."

"No problem," she went on to say, "but you are gonna owe me big! They are still putting together the last house you and Pepper borrowed!"

"It's not like that this time, I promise."

"OK, swing by, I'll get you a key."

"Thanks Kim, 'preciate it."

I hung up, with a plan in mind. "Janet, you take Ruth and the kids in her car and meet me at the liquor store across from the entrance to the park in Lake Elsinore."

"Pepper, I need some stuff from the house."

"What about the cops?" He asked.

"You're a smart guy bro prowl and growl, do you still have the combination to the safe?"

"Why are you still here?" I inquired in my usual smart-ass tone.

CHAPTER 20
SAFE HOUSE

All I could think of on my way to Elsinore, what my wife and Ruth could possibly be talking about. It made me shiver. Janet has made certain accusations about my friendliness toward Ruth.

"Try not to think about it," I told myself. "You have bigger fish to fry. Okay, so, who would go to these lengths to erase us like this? It's almost like a test to see how good we are. I can't buy that, someone wants us dead, they just haven't sent the right guys.....yet."

Things just were not going well for me, I had three dead bodies all traceable to me, and a page from Pepper, Don't use the freeway the cops are looking for you, love P. Oh yeah, let's not forget the fact my wife was sitting in the car with a woman she assumes I am sleeping with. "How much more shit could possibly get dumped on me?" I asked myself.

"Fuckin' A."

I ducked off Fairview just before the HQ of the Costa Mesa Police Department. I pulled my bike into the church parking lot and cut off the engine. I needed a minute to catch my breath and calm myself down. "Relax," I said to myself, "the bike is registered to a ghost, don't speed, no problem. Right? Right."

Talking to myself was the easiest way to see a problem and a possible solution. I fired up the Harley once more and slid out onto Fair Drive East, right past the police station. I couldn't resist the urge, and flipped the bird at the building as I drove by at thirty miles per hour. Granted I was a cop, but these guys were looking for me!

Merging onto the 55 North Freeway, I found myself blending with all the other commuters heading for Lake Elsinore.

Janet broke the silence once the kids had fallen asleep in the back seat. "How long?" She asked Ruth.

131

Ruth looked at her and quietly said, "five, six months I guess."

"Have you slept with him?" Janet tightened her hands on the steering wheel, fighting the tears and the anger.

"No!"

The answer surprised and startled Janet. This was way too much to deal with in one day. Janet had no idea what her husband really did in his other job. His other world. All she knew, it wasn't like his police work.

Janet had met Rowdy four years ago at the Sheriffs Academy. He was the class wise-ass who would sit next to a friend of his, who wasn't much better. Wherever Rowdy was, Troy wasn't far behind. They were inseparable, the best of friends. Then the rivalry began-over her. She tried to calm her racing heart, remembering that night. The fight the two had because of her. Troy and Rowdy never spoke again after that night. It would be difficult for Troy to speak ever again anyway, even back then Rowdy liked to go for the throat. That was when she first learned what Rowdy was capable of. It should have scared the hell out of her, and it did. But she also felt safe with him.

As they traveled south on the 15 Freeway, Janet wondered where Rowdy learned to kill with such precision. "I guess he really did go to all those training sessions, instead of going to her like I thought," she thought to herself.

"I've misjudged him," Janet said quietly.

"You need to tell him that, not me," Ruth countered, "he loves you, you know.

"He loves you too. That's the problem," Janet answered. Yet, she didn't have the same defeated voice. She saw her husband in a different light, but she still had some unanswered questions regarding his faithfulness to her.

"At least you wear his ring, you have something to show for it. I have an empty bed and a few phone calls."

"When he goes on assignment, that's all I have too."

Ruth waited a moment before replying, and with resignation in her voice, "That may be, but he comes home to you."

A trip to Rowdy's house in Colton, was marred only by the southern California traffic. The cops were watching the house, but that was expected. Pepper drove by and turned left at the corner, parked and hopped out of the truck. He checked his six as he went over the fence, found the spare key in the power box, and was inside of the house within four-seconds.

As he moved down the hallway, he pulled his Ruger from its holster and entered the bedroom. He knew he couldn't use the light, no sense alerting Johnny Law. He would just have to go by what little light trickled in through the window. He made his way to the wall, opened the hidden access panel exposing the safe, and went to work. Pepper had committed the combination to memory, but it was more fun cracking the code with the lights off. With a soft click, he gained access.

"Not bad, forty-eight seconds," Pepper said to himself, "but not a personal best." Once inside, he extracted the necessary equipment he thought would be needed, and closed the safe. He crossed the room to the closet and opened it reaching for the hidden slide out that would produce the SKS Sportster 7.62 thumbhole stock that Rowdy had converted to full auto.

He set all of this on the bed as he grabbed clothes for both Rowdy and Janet, throwing them into a suitcase. He tossed the suitcase and supplies over the fence into the cab of his truck, jumped back over, and casually drove away. While reaching for a CD to listen to, he chuckled to himself, "too easy."

A brief visit to Kim was all I could spare. It wasn't time to play catch up, and how is your life? Besides that, I was a married man with more than enough trouble waiting for me down the road. "Man, she is a looker too," I thought to myself, "and gullible. Gotta love it!"

By the time Janet and Ruth pulled up beside me, I could tell they were getting antsy. I shouted, "We're all set, let's go." With Janet following me, we made our way to the house Kim lent me. It was a large two-story that backed next to the waters edge. Two boats were parked at the slip at the end of the wooden dock.

"Nice huh?" I asked sheepishly to anyone who cared to listen.

Janet was definitely not in the mood for my bragging, and said, "I have to call mom. Thank God she had the kids tonight. I need to let her know to keep em for a while at Arrowhead for a while till she hears from us."

I handed her the cell phone and walked toward Ruth. "So, how pissed is she and what did you tell her?" I asked Ruth, directly. I wasn't in the mood for games, and needed to know if I still had a marriage.

"Not very much, and I don't know how pissed off she is," Ruth replied.

"This is only temporary Ruth, but everybody is going to have to get along until I can get this sorted out."

I called Pepper, and with instructions to him, and a few wisecracks from him, he showed up about ten minutes later with everything pilfered from my house.

Pepper whistled, "Nice digs, how'd ya manage this?" He asked.

"Kim said the people who live here are in Spain for a year, so we'll be safe here for some time." Both of us knew that safe was a relative term, but the house would buy us some time to get our bearings and take steps to improve our position. I didn't want to stay here too long, that much was certain.

We dined on a gourmet meal of pizza, buffalo wings and Dos Equis, Pepper and my favorite. Of course, if you asked me, the hotter the better on the wings. It goes without saying, the beer better be ice cold. Everyone settled in for the evening, and our first night was like we were one big happy family. Okay, so were weren't so happy.

"I'll take the first watch," Pepper volunteered, as he headed out the door. See ya in about four hours." I nodded to him, as he smiled at me. Leaving me alone with both Janet and Ruth. As I turned away from him, I came face to face with Janet.

"We need to talk." Her voice had taken on an urgency I hadn't heard very often in all our time together.

"About what?" I asked, trying to make it seem as if everything was fine and hunky dory.

"Rowdy, I'm not gonna play games with you tonight, too much has happened to us today. I....I..."

"You what?" I questioned, my tone matching hers.

"I'm afraid of losing you if I'm not careful."

I knew she was talking about Ruth, but I wasn't going to go there. "You're not gonna lose me, Pepper an' me kin handle this." My normally hidden New York accent was leaking out. I usually try to hide it, but I was too tired. I didn't even bother trying to from her. She had to have been able to see it in my face.

"Forget it Row, I can see you are exhausted, besides you have to relieve your brother in four hours. Get some rest....I love you."

She leaned up on tiptoe and kissed me on the cheek, with an extra squeeze on my hand, and walked away. I flopped over to the couch. Yes, I was exhausted and my body hurt. I managed to drift off into a deep sleep, with the days events playing in my head as I did.

The morning sun pierced through the uneven slits of the blinds that covered the massive sliding glass door, and the rays played across my face. I could feel its warmth, but couldn't quite make it out of that world of the unconscious. It had to be easy to see everything about me in that light. I knew the scars, and lines on my face well. The pain in the scars left by a raving psychopath wielding a straight razor. I had done my job well and the client lived to tell his grand kids about it.

Meanwhile, I had spent two days in intensive care, courtesy of a staff infection from the rusty blade. The lines were deep, and not just from scars. I felt I was getting old. Not quite the kid I used to be, and even getting a bit thin on top. I worked extra hard to keep the shape that came easily to me five years before. Make no mistake, I am in great shape, the perfect machine as I have been referred to by my peers. I could go days on end with little or no sleep and still provide my client with better protection than anyone else in the biz. Pepper, I knew, envied me. He was the next best thing to me, and knew it. I never rubbed his face in that, an it was probably a main reason why Pepper would do anything for me. Including dying if necessary.

I couldn't avoid it anymore. Consciousness was coming, and I couldn't stop it. I cracked open an eye, lifted up my left arm and checked my G-Shock for time. O-light hundred. He opened the other eye, and Pepper and Ruth came into full view.

"Why didn't ya'll wake me up?" I asked, feeling guilty.

"I figured you could use the rest. Besides Janet took over for me at 0300," said Pepper.

"You let Janet take a watch? Are you crazy?" I shouted.

"You got a problem with that?" Asked Janet.

I spun around to see her walking across the kitchen toward me, and giving me a glare that just dared me to say something against her. "I just don't think it's such a good idea for you to be out there all by yourself," I said, lowering my voice.

"Well, with a virtual army of people out there trying to kill us, we figured you could use all the help you could get." She said with a smirk.

I hate it when she talks down to me like that, but she was also right, and I couldn't fight her on that one. The day was shaping up to be a winner. "I gotta make some phone calls, so if ya'll could leave me alone for a while......?" I wasn't about to explain it all to them, but they respected my wishes and slowly walked out of the room. I offered a smile and wink to Janet, to let her know I appreciated her help.

Pepper started to get all the weapons ready. A quick count of ammunition and the decision was made for him to make a run for supplies.

"There's an indoor shooting range in Temecula. That's the closest place I know," said Pepper.

Leave it up to Pepper to know where every gun store in a twenty mile radius is, no matter where he is. Pepper made up our wish list: 1,000 rounds .45 acp Remington Golden Saber in +P+, 2,000 rounds 9 mm 124 grain Golden Saber, 100 rounds 7.62 x 39 Winchester Fail Safe, 2,000 rounds 7.62 x 39 FMJ, 500 rounds 12 gauge double 00 buck, 2 cans smokeless powder, 2 boxes magnum primers, 200 Speer Gold Dots hollow points .45 acp, 500 Speer Gold Dots hollow points 9 mm.

"With what we got now, this oughta give us in the neighborhood of 8,000 rounds, ya think that'll be enough?" Pepper asked, more serious than joking.

"How much Semtex did you say I have?" I asked.
"'Bout six condoms worth," Pepper answered.

"What about cord?"

"Plenty!" Pepper hollered over his shoulder as he walked toward the door.

"We're gonna need some batteries for the phones and radios!" I yelled, as he closed the front door.

CHAPTER 21
5 MILLIONS REASONS

Ponce was actually quite amused by the mess I seemed to have gotten myself in. He invited myself and the clan to head down to Nasty City, the name we affectionately called a small community outside of San Diego, to stay with him. It wouldn't be as well protected as his personal version of Attica, but Ponce knew security, so I knew we would be as safe as was possible.

"And Rowdy? I got all the dies and a brand new Dillon Machine that will do everything but suck your cock."

"Thanks Ponce, we should be there a little before sundown," I answered.

"Via Con Dios Amigo." Then Ponce Signed off.

Pepper finally showed up, about three hours after he left. He had everything I requested and more. "I took the liberty of gettin' us some Chinese food, hope ya'll are hungry," he said with a big grin.

I hadn't given it much thought, but once I could smell that pungent, almost throat choking aroma of sweet and sour chicken wafting in the air, I realized I had a voracious appetite.

Pepper and I separated ourselves from the rest of the group, and exchanged information we both gathered separately throughout the day. It didn't really amount to much, and nothing could be determined by any of it. We decided to concentrate on making plans to move all of us south.

Once dinner was over with, the house became a bustle of activity. I stowed as much equipment and essentials as I could in my saddlebags on my Iron Horse, Pepper put much of the gear in his truck. Janet and Ruth put away the rest in the trunk of Ruth's Forest Green 1996 Ford Taurus.

I roughed out a map to Ponce's house, so if we happened to get separated, everyone would at least know how to get to his place. Janet kissed me gently on the lips and with a last squeeze of my hand, got into the car. I started up the Harley, and shouted over the uneven loping of the big twin engine between my legs, "Don't stop for anything!"

I motioned for everyone to switch on their Motorola radios, all three gave a thumbs up.

"Check, check, check....can everyone hear me?"

"Loud and clear here bro," said Pepper.

"Here too," piped in Janet.

"Me too," replied Ruth.

We set off in somewhat of a convoy form, and it took us nine minutes to get to the ramp at Railroad Canyon. So far so good. I knew that once we got onto the freeway, we would be in the safest place possible. Someone would be pretty hard pressed to get our convoy stopped at sixty-five MPH, with bumper to bumper traffic.

The black Chevy Suburban moved quietly down the private driveway. It stopped halfway and let out eight passengers all dressed in black and carrying H & K MP5 suppressed machine guns. Each man moved with precision, careful not to disturb the ground and make any unnecessary noise, alerting the guards. In minutes it was over. The private army had neutralized everyone on the grounds and entered the main house. It was clear: grab the president and CEO of TBP without injuring him and get out before the police arrive.

The man who led this well-oiled machinery of men said to himself, "Piece of cake. These men are the best." He was in constant contact with his group, and they let him know what was going on, while he watched the time. Selecting a replacement for the man inadvertently killed wasn't easy. There were few precious companies that supply the government directly. Even fewer that can

140

by-pass customs.

"Managed properly, there will be no problems importing my own product," he mused to himself.

He checked his watch, six minutes after breaching the perimeter, all nine passengers were back in the suburban heading up the driveway back the way they came in. They passed a long line of Toyota's with blue flashing lights and hi-low sirens careening down the narrow two lane country road.

Their precious cargo lay on the floor bound and gagged in the fetal position, zipped up in a black oversize duffle. He made no movements. He didn't dare to. I heard my cell phone ring, and pushing the three position to P, I answered, "Rowdy!"

"Mr. Calhoun?" The voice was definitely Japanese.

"What can I do for you?" I asked cautiously.

"My name is Furusho Yokohama, and I have a need for your services. Is this a good time?"

"Give me your number, I will call you back in ten minutes."

"Hai, arigato," he said, and furnished me with his phone number.

I slid the switch back to R, then keyed my mike to talk to Pepper. "Pep, I need to use the Sat phone, pull over."

"There's an Arco Station up head in Rainbow, ETA four minutes! Can you wait till then Row?"

Janet chimed in, "Ruth's kids gotta pee!"

"Okay, everyone off at the next exit!" I said. Two 10-4's later, we pulled into the gas station. We gassed up all the vehicles, got some coffee and snacks, and I pulled off to a little side road from the

141

station to make a long distance phone call.

"Mr. Yokohama?" I asked the voice that picked up on the other end.

"Mr. Calhoun, are you available for a very important assignment?" Mr Yokohama asked.

"What seems to be the problem?" I could clearly hear the distress in his voice.

"Approximately four hours ago, Mr. Toshio Akimura, the President of TBP Corporation was kidnapped."

"What does this have to do with me? I'm an executive protection specialist."

"Mr. Calhoun," Mr Yokohama went on to say, "you are too modest. The kidnappers specifically ordered us not to cooperate with the police, otherwise they will kill Mr. Akimura."

"Mr. Yokohama, what do you want from me?"

"The kidnappers want twenty-million dollars, that is American dollars for his safe release. I have been authorized by the board of directors to pay this amount. However we are not equipped to deal with a hostage situation.

"Mr. Yokohama, I do not do that kind of work anymore, besides there are plenty of operatives who you can buy to handle this situation."

"Mr. Calhoun, Richard Allbright said you were the best."

"What the fuck?" I said to myself. "Why isn't Dick handling your problem?" I asked.

"He is in Panama handling a problem for their government, he recommended you highly."

I was taking all this in. Something just didn't quite jive with me. Allbright hated me, this much I knew. Why he would send business my way, was beyond me. I glanced over at Pepper, and he was busy making ching-ching sounds, nodding his head yes to take the gig.

"Mr. Calhoun, we are prepared to pay you five million American plus expenses to handle this problem....the board wants Mr. Akimura back, unharmed. We will send a private jet for you and your team."

"I'll get back with you in about four hours Mr. Yokohama."

"Konichi-wa, Mr. Calhoun."

I replaced the receiver in its cradle, folded up the antennae and closed the case. I just sat there staring at the phone....thinking.

"The thang about it is, we can retire after this job!" Said Pepper after I told him what the payoff would be. Pepper was right. We could retire, possibly start our own protection consulting company, just like we had talked about. I would have to think about it a later, we had other matters that needed to be dealt with right then and there.

CHAPTER 22
PONCE

We arrived at Ponce's house shortly before 1800 hours. As a courtesy and to show his usual hospitality, he had stocked the fridge with our favorite double XX brand beer, which by the way he greeted us with at the door.

"Hi honey, I'm home!" Said Pepper as he took his beer.

I took mine and with a grin said, "Much obliged to ya."

Ponce strained to see past my body, toward our vehicles, as Janet pulled in. "You startin' a home for wayward victims of crime or what?" He inquired. "Who are......?"

Before Ponce could finish his question, he recognized the short dark hair and diminutive stature of my assumed extramarital interest.

"Are you fuckin' nuts Rowdy? What is she doin' here? Does Janet know? Jeeeezus Christ!"

"Ponce, what the hell is this, twenty questions? I had no choice, they sent a team to kidnap her and trap me!"

"Janet is gonna wear your balls for earrings," Ponce said in disbelief.

Ponce was fighting back the laughter, and I poked him in the ribs. My way of telling him to shut the hell up.

Pepper was trying to fight back his laugh, and couldn't contain himself, "Why don't you ask her Ponce? She's in the car with Ruth!"

He saw the look I threw at him, and Pepper quickly got his composure back. Ponce on the other hand, wasn't doing so well. He kept looking at me, then to Ruth then to Janet. He would get this look on his face, shake his head and just mutter, "Jeezus Christ."

Pepper leaned against the porch wall, and took a long healthy pull of his beer. I followed suit, then Ponce finally realized we were in some serious shit. "How long you need to stash them?" He asked.

"Well, that's the problem. I don't know. I got a call about an hour ago from Japan. Seems there is a hostage situation involving a high ranking official of a large corporation."

Ponce just full of questions or comments, "I thought you didn't do that anymore." He tried to tread lightly on this subject. He knew that I was part of an Op that didn't go well at all. Ponce, besides Pepper and myself, were the only members of the HRT that came out of it alive. We lost the rest of the team members and most of the hostages. I was in charge of that Op, and still felt responsible for those deaths. It was the reason I got out of that shit. Too much responsibility, too many variables....too much guilt.

"I don't," I replied, "but everyone else is busy. Allbright is in Panama and I already know Roger is still down in Argentina on the oil rigs."

"Rowdy? How do you know where Allbright is?" Ponce asked.

"According to one Mr. Yokohama, he recommended me for this job, and Yokohama told me of his location."

"It's not that you aren't good or nothin' like that Rowdy, but Richard recommending you doesn't sit well. I mean, he fuckin' hates you. Why would he tell someone you're the best for the job?"

"So whatcha sayin?" I growled with a smile.

He just sighed with resignation, "So, whatcha gonna do?"

"Pepper must be a terrible poker player," I thought to myself. By his face, I could understand why, the interest in my answer was written all over it.

"Where's Pepper?" I asked to anyone who might know and

would answer. Ponce motioned to the den where an entire wall of small TV screens gave a commanding view of all five acres Ponce owned, walking Rowdy toward them.

"There," he said, pointing to a thermal image on a separate, larger screen, indicating Peppers exact location on a grid. "The screen is set up so that when you look at it, it shows the relative location in relation to your position."

"Plain English please."

"If you face the screen, and he is here," Ponce pointed to three o'clock, "it means he is on your right, simple even for you."

"Smart ass. What about defenses?"

"Also simple, even for you. See all the blue dots on the screen?"

Ponce was referring to the hundred or so dots all over the screen. "Claymores?" I asked.

"Yup, they're electrically activated by this button and deactivated by pressing this button." He showed me each button, and even made a post-it-note for me, so I wouldn't get confused. How sweet of him. If I really feel the need, I can detonate them one by one just by touching the dot on the screen. Cool huh?"

"Fuckin' A!" What else was there for me to say?

"I can also activate it like a car alarm!" With this key fob, when I leave the grounds, I can get em all lit up like a Christmas tree. I really hate intruders."

"I can tell." The devilish grin on Ponce's face was one of his trademarks.

"If everything goes as planned, Rowdy Calhoun, and his band of merry men, will be in Japan in less than thirty-six hours."

"What if he doesn't take the job?" Said a raspy voiced man, standing at parade rest near the television.

"He'll take it, don't worry. He'll take it." The man lit a Marlboro. "He'll take it," he said to his reflection in the window of his hotel room overlooking downtown Tokyo.

CHAPTER 23
TEMPER, TEMPER

As I leaned closer to the mirror, I saw how tired my eyes looked. This was enhanced by the fine lines that have made their presence known around them. While going through the morning events in my head, I decided to at least make a concerted effort to do something with the stuff growing on my face. After running my hand over three days worth of stubble, I decide on a goatee, and used the electric shaver.

"Nice look!" Teased Janet, as I walked into the kitchen.

"You like?" I asked.

She came to me and gently ran her hand over my chin, noticing for the first time the gray I was beginning to accumulate. "Look's like someone's gettin' old," she chided.

"Who you callin' old?" I replied, using as deep of Peppers drawl as I could muster to better accentuate my displeasure of being teased about my age.

"You, is who! You're older than me and that's all that counts," Janet said with a laugh.

"Can we talk about something else, please?" My demeanor went from playful to serious in about the time it takes to blink an eye. I just didn't have it in me for anymore grab ass. "There's business to discuss, and I'd like to do it before I get any older!"

"What's up boss?" Asked Pepper.

We noticed Ponce staring at the plate Janet sat before him.

"Something wrong?" Janet asked him.

"It's just that I haven't had any home cookin' in quite some time, and I'm afraid it's gonna be a shock to my system."

"No body likes a smart ass Ponce," Janet said with a slightly irritated voice and swift brain duster to the back of the head.

"Okay everybody," I began, "listen up. I've got a plan." I reached for the ashtray, and Pepper tossed my cigarettes from off the counter. He hoisted himself up, lit a Marlboro, and let me know he was all ears. "Some of this is gonna be good, some of it isn't."

Lifting an eyebrow and squinting through the smoke, I looked at Janet said, "Everybody understand?"

She looked unhappy, but nodded yes. During the course of our marriage, she knew when she could argue with me, and when she couldn't. She knew this was a couldn't moment. "Here's the deal kids. Japan is antsy for us to come and take care of this little problem. Ponce, you're gonna stay here and keep an eye on the girls. Am I correct in the understanding that everyone will be safe here?"

"Rowdy, you're gonna need me on this," Ponce replied, "besides, the compound runs itself. All they've got to do, is remember not to step on the land mines after they've been set." Ponce sat back, thinking he had talked his way into coming on the assignment, when he said, "Hey, we're missin' somebody.

Pepper stuck his thumb out and gestured behind him toward the foyer, "She's out..."

"Oh shit, God dammit Pepper!" Shouted Ponce

"Sorry, I wasn't thinking!" He answered back, and followed Ponce out of the kitchen.

I was really getting pissed off, "Somebody find her before she kills herself!"

Ponce ran into the den with Pepper and I behind him. He found the quarry he sought on the scanning screen. "She's on the driveway, between the trucks." He said. Pepper was ready to volunteer to get Ruth, when Pepper grabbed him back. "Just cause she was a lucky idiot, doesn't mean you will be too."

Ponce picked up the chrome freestanding microphone, flicked the switch on his massive control panel and spoke. "Ruth, do not move..."

"Just shut the fucking system down! Jesus Christ, how hard is that?" I shouted.
Once the system has been activated by what it thinks is a hostile invader, I can't override it just like that."

"Meatwhistle?!"

"I planted them, I know where they are. I will get her. Everyone else just stay in the house. The neighbors really get pissed when these things go off."

I stared at the screen. Thermo-imaging allowed me to watch the heat from their bodies. One moving cautiously, the other, frozen in place. Pepper stood in the doorway holding his breath, and Janet likewise sat still, waiting to see what happened.

I turned on his sounds, to hear what he was saying," Just stay where you are, everything is gonna be just fine. Don't move a muscle Ruth. Don't shift your weight. If you can help it, don't even breath."

What in reality felt like eternity, amounted to about 40 seconds when Ponce finally reached Ruth. We were hoping for the same outcome, and I heard a whisper from Janet, that rocked me to my soul. "Let the bitch die." I knew I had to get this Ruth thing resolved, as soon as I had a few minutes without someone trying to kill me. Right then and there, wasn't the time, seconds felt like minutes, minutes felt like hours, and selfishly I thought, "I really don't need any new challenges in my life."

I went to the window to watch Ponce's progress. I could see him crouch on hands and keens and press down on the rubber covered button in the tail cap of his Surefire8X, illuminating the

150

ground at Ruth's feet. Her natural reaction must have been to step back, because that is what she looked as if she were about to do. Ponce reached out and grabbed her by the belt line. "Where the hell do you think you're going?" He demanded. "I told you not to move.

"What....what are you looking for?" Asked Ruth.

"Sneaker Patrol ma'am," replied Ponce in his usual wisecracking manner.

Ever since I have known him, he always dealt with stress by being a smart ass. The more jokes he told, the more stress he was under. The wisecracks were just his way of blowing it off.

"If you must know," Ponce went on, "I am trying to make sure you aren't standing on a land mine." He poked and probed at the ground with his dinner fork. "Shit!"

"What's the...the....matter?" Ruth asked Ponce

"I hate not being prepared," he answered.

"I thought you guys were always prepared. Like the Boy Scouts."

"Yeah, well," continued Ponce with a chuckle, "not during dinner, it was my night off. Okay, you're clean." Ponce held four fingers in the air, indicating Code 4 to Pepper. Pepper called it out to me.

Ponce grabbed Ruth around the waist, picked her up and placed her on the hood of the truck.

"That's not paid for yet!" Shouted Pepper.

Ponce jumped up on the hood with Ruth, and waited fifteen-seconds and stabbed one of the buttons on the remote with his thumb. The house lights blinked off, then on. He slid off the truck onto the gravel driveway, extending his arm for Ruth to follow. I could hear that conversation that transpired between them, which only further fueled the anger I already felt.

"You cannot, I repeat, cannot wander out of this house without telling somebody where you are going. Do I make myself clear?" His tone was serious, the smile gone from his face. Waiting for an answer, he stopped, putting his arms across his chest.

"Crystal," she replied with a wavering chin. Her face covered in obvious fright and embarrassment for what she was going through.

"I don't give a rat's fuck about your personal problems, but the lives of my team members and what is more important, my friends come first. You become lonely. Understood?"

Ruth numbly nodded.

That was not good enough for Ponce "Understand?!" He shouted.

As he did so, Ruth not only jumped, but so did Pepper and I. We weren't used to this display from Ponce, and it was quite intense.

"Yes, I understand. I...I'm sorry."

"You need to get back into the house, and find something to occupy your time." Ponce walked behind Ruth, back to the house. I could see his inhale and slow exhale, as he attempted to get a grip.

I was waiting for them in the foyer. Ruth was the first to reach me, and found herself thrown about four feet in the air, as my hand met with her face. She landed in a corner, slumped and with a bloody lip. Both Pepper and Ponce made a step to stop me, but I let them know that would not be a good choice at that moment. "Who the fuck do you think you are?" I demanded from her.

"And what the fuck do you think you are doing?" I glanced around me a moment, and saw the look of shock on their faces. Janet's really caught me off guard. In all the years we have known each other, and all the arguments we have had, I have never once raised my hand to her. "I think you're confusing our friendship with my loyalty to my team. Do it again, and they will be finding pieces of you in five states."

Pepper tried to talk, but I silenced him with a look, and said, "I don't fuckin' want to hear it!" My voice went up about another two octaves, "Now, we have work to do. Everybody in the God damn kitchen"! "I'm FUCKIN DONE"!

I sat down at the table, and Janet set two fingers of tequila in front of me. "Now, where was I before we were so rudely interrupted?"

Ponce chimed in with, "You were tellin' me how lucky you were to have me as your friend."

Pepper leaned over to him, touching his shoulder. I could hear his whispers, "The thang about it is, I don't think he's in the mood."

Ponce nodded, "Sorry Row, as you were."

"Ponce, what time do we have to leave here to be at Brown Field by 0700?

"0630," he replied.

"Okay, plan on leaving tomorrow at 0500. As I started to say to Ponce, I want the girls to stay here. Do not let them out of your sight for any reason."

"And like I said," argued Ponce, "you are going to need me on this detail."

"Didn't I just say, I wasn't in the mood?" I growled in reply.

CHAPTER 24
TEMPER, TEMPER

Just as I was about to argue my case with Ponce the damn phone rang. How many more interruptions would I have to put up with? "this better be good," I answered gruffly.

"Rowdy Calhoun?" An unknown voice queried.

"Yeah, what did I win?"

"Mr. Calhoun, will we be enjoying your company in Japan?" The digitally altered voices I heard were undistinguishable.

I looked over at Ponce, and mouthed, "Can this call be traced?" He motioned for me to follow him and we rushed to the den. Ponce slipped another phone into a cradle, punched a few numbers at his keyboard and gestured for me to look at a screen. This one had a map on it covering Conus.

Ponce made circles in the air with this index finger, "Keep em talkin,'" he whispered.

I cupped the receiver of my cell phone and mouthed, "How long?"

He shrugged, "I don't know, twenty maybe thirty-seconds."

"Who wants to know?" I asked my new friend. "How did you get this number?"

"That is not important," was the response. What should be important to you, is the safety of your family and your friends."

"Who the fuck is this?" I demanded. "Stop playin' games, if you got something to say, say it!"

"Let's just say if you were to come to Japan, you're personal

154

troubles would be over."

"And I'm sure an upstandin' citizen such as yourself is one hundred percent trustworthy, huh?" I inquired, wasting time for Ponce's trace.

"I give you my word of honor, besides, if I wanted in that compound in National City, I would be in." Even though the voice was digitized, it still had a smug sound to it.

I looked at Ponce with a frown, as he showed me what was going on. "He's bouncing his fuckin' signal off three satellites. Look, you can see it on the screen. London, Switzerland, Thailand, India, it keeps moving, I can't lock it."

"Having fun Ponce?" Asked the chuckling electronic voice. "I can bounce this signal off of any satellite I wish and keep you looking all day long."

"What do you want from me?" I demanded.

"I am merely extending an invitation for you to enjoy the Orient," was the answer.

"And I am supposed to let everybody go their separate ways and not have to worry about my wife and kids while I am there?"

"That is correct, I have no interest in anyone but yourself. I will see you in Japan." The call abruptly ended.

"God dammit, fuck, shit!!" I shouted in rage and frustration, then threw the cell phone across the room. It shattered into about a million pieces.

Shaking his head, Ponce said, "The guy you buy those from must be putting his kids through college because of you."

Not in the mood to spar, I continued, "How many available members for the team?" I looked at the sensor screens, making sure no one was trying to outflank us.

"I don't know for sure. Five, six, maybe seven at the most. On this short of notice, you're lucky to get that," he answered.

"Who's available?"

"Well, I have already done some checking, and Ted, Mike and Philip say they want to go."

"Is that all?" I asked. My voice full of disappointment.

"I'm still waiting on two more answers," Ponce added with optimism.

"Leave messages Ponce, tell em if they can be at the plane at 0630, they have a job. Otherwise, we go with what we've got."

"Roger that."

I headed to the kitchen while Ponce continued with his necessary phone calls. I could tell Janet was upset, but I wasn't in the mood to argue with her. That would come later...if there was a later. I looked around the kitchen, and saw Ruth's head held cradled in her arms on the table. I looked at Pepper, and he nodded an affirmative to let me know she was asleep.

"Everybody get some shuteye," I said, "we will reconvene at 0500 here."

Again Pepper nodded, and I headed for the back patio to get some fresh air. I didn't realize it, but Janet was hot on my heels.

"Rowdy!" Called Janet.

I could see her reflection in the sliding glass door that led from the kitchen to the small fenced area complete with hot tub, shower stall and pool. She didn't look happy, and I really didn't want to talk to her about all of this. As I opened the sliding door, my nostrils flared at that heavily sweet chlorine smell of the pool hanging in the dense night air.

"Rowdy!" She repeated in a more firm tone.

I turned around and faced her, "Look Janet, I know you're worried, but this is the last one. This is my chance to finally be through with this kind of living."

"Rowdy, you have told me that at least three other times!"

"It's different this time Janet."

"Bullshit!" She shouted, as her anger rose. It's the same as every other time you promised."

"Honey, I'm serious, this time it's different."

"Tell me Rowdy, what makes this job any different from any other?"

"The money!" My tone rose to slightly above hers.

"Rowdy, how many times do I have to tell you, I don't care about the money?"

"You don't understand, this is the last job. They're gonna pay me five million plus expenses to handle this assignment."

"Five million?" She asked, slightly stunned with the amount.

"What, you don't think I'm worth it?" I asked, sounding defensive.

"No, it isn't that. I can't believe they would pay that on top of the ransom."

"They said it's imperative they get the president back."

"How long do you think you will be gone this time?" Janet

asked, as she crossed her arms over her chest. She knew the typical answer was coming.

"Shouldn't take more than..."

"Seventy-two hours?" She said, finishing my answer.

"Uh...yeah, plus travel time, give or take..."

"A few?"

She did it again. "Dammit, knock it off!" More softly I continued, "Am I really that bad?"

"Yes!!"

"I gotta do this, okay?"

"And I gotta do this Rowdy. I won't be here when you get back. I'm gettin' the kids and going to the mountains. Come find me when you get back home."

She left me standing out there, alone with my thoughts. "Fuckin' women. Can't live with em, can't shoot em!" I said out loud.

"Depends on what country you're in bro." Pepper stood in the open doorway.

"What?" I asked. Not really coherent as to what he was talkin' about.

"Time for shut eye. Come on."

I couldn't fight it anymore. It had been roughly 18 hours since my last nap, and it was only 2000 hours. "Thanks Pep, I'm turnin' in."

As I stretched out next to Janet, feeling her warm body against me, she rolled over placing her leg over mine, and wrapping her arm across my chest and squeezed tightly. I whispered I love you, kissed her gently on the forehead and closed my eyes. I felt sleep taking me quickly, but could feel Janet's warm fingers, smoothing the few chest hairs I had.

When Janet woke the next morning, it was to silence. She reached across the bed, searching for Rowdy, with one arm outstretched and eyes still closed. She was alone. She drew back her arm and pulled herself deeper into the covers, and chewed silently on her lower lip to keep from crying.

Brown field, San Diego, California 0545 Hours

Pepper and I stood shoulder to shoulder looking out of the private hangar. "Nice sunrise, huh?" Asked Pepper.

"I've seen better," I answered quietly.

"How long you think this is gonna take?" He inquired.

"I figure we should have everything loaded in about an hour and fifteen minutes."

"No Rowdy, this little hop and pop."

"I don't know, seventy-two hours hopefully." I thought to myself, "If everything goes right." I reached into my pocket for my Oakley's, the sun was beginning to shine brightly. You could see the heat rising off the tarmac.

"Hey! It would be nice to have some help over here!" Ponce screamed from across the hangar deck.

"Pep, give him a hand, wouldya? I will keep watch to see who shows." I pulled the brim of my Wrangler size 7 3/8 black wool cowboy hat down a little lower to compensate for the rising sun, a gift from my brother while on a bodyguard gig in Taos, New Mexico. I could barely make out a fast, approaching vehicle. As the vehicle got closer, I could hear music. The closer it got, the louder it became.

159

"God damn, that's gotta be Phil," I said to myself.

Ponce didn't even bother to look up to check, "Here comes M.C.!" He yelled.

Jeez, how does he do that? As the vehicle came within fifteen feet, I motioned for him to pull into the hangar. The music was deafening. Ponce, Pepper and myself all approached his car to admire the sound system. You know us boys with our toys. Phil cut the engine and stepped out of the car, music still booming in the hangar. As he walked away from his vehicle, the music followed him. "What the fuck?" I said in amazement.

Phil reached into his pocket and pulled out his Walkman, then pushed a button to stop. All it once it was deadly quiet.

"The thang about it is...." Pepper began, "You're gonna go fuckin' deaf listenin' to shit like that."

"Keeps me focused, Yahoo and Yahoo."

"I figured it for at least 250 watts Phil," I said, still impressed with the decibels.

Phil opened the boot of his Porsche and grabbed his bags. He walked under the wing and dropped them at the foot of the steps. "Hey Ponce!" He shouted, "Who's in charge of this mission?" Ponce grinned, and gestured with his head in my direction.

Pepper stood in front of him, blocking out the sunlight. "That gonna be a problem for you?" He asked.

"Nah, I got no problem with Rowdy, that was all Richard, remember?"

CHAPTER 25
COLD NOODLES AND WARM PUSSY

We arrived at Tokyo airport without incident. All of us were pretty tired due to the fact we had so much work to do on the plane, reports don't get written by themselves and I cant remember the last time I saw a gun clean itself and put itself away.

As we deplaned a representative of TFB corporation met us at the bottom of the stairs, I thought I recognized him, it had been three years since I saw Toshio last. He had done very well for himself, climbing the corporate ladder all the way up to the VP rung. I was the first one off the plane, Toshio and I bowed to each other he waved his hand in the air and in moments a small tractor-like looking vehicle appeared along with several men in blue jumpsuits and adorable blue hardhats that actually had a shine, they opened the cargo hold and began unloading the contents placing them ever so carefully onto the trailer behind the tug. The men worked quietly and in unison completing their task quickly and efficiently.

Toshio walked us toward the terminal ground entrance, he guided us through the maze of red tape and bullshit known as customs, speaking rapid fire Japanese at the agents behind the counter and in less than an hour we were in a motorcade of private vehicles and headed toward the hotel.

Toshio and I occupied the backseat of the lead car. He lit a cigarette and began smoking without rolling the window down. As I cracked the window to get some fresh air, he broke the silence. "It is very good to see you Rowdy-San." His command of the English language was much improved from the last time we met. "Hai, Domo Arigato, Toshio-San. It is good to see you too!" "How have you been?" He smiled and finished his cigarette after the customary small talk, we drove the rest of the way in silence to the hotel.

Everything was going according to plan. I'm sure something is wrong somewhere I thought. Toshio told me that the men in jumpsuits would be taking our gear to the hotel while we were on our way to meet a very nervous VPOTC. Toshio also explained he had made arrangements with the police for us to carry our weapons while in Japan. This is a good thing I thought, as weapons of any kind are expressly forbidden in Japan. "The permits will be delivered to us at Corporate Headquarters at 0800 sharp." Toshio said looking confidant. And why shouldn't he. This is a country founded on principals of promptness. The very thought that it wouldn't happen would cause an embarrassing situation. So 0800 it would be. I'm patient.

The VPOTC presided over the meeting like a queen over her court. The employees resembling busy little worker bees scurrying about; pushing papers in front of her to sign, approve this, schedule that. Once in a while she would nod her head in disapproval. At that point the man standing in front of her at that time would change color from a mild tan to a pale white. It was all very amusing to watch. I on the other hand was not to be bullied or threatened. The board of directors asked me to be here, not the other way around. After sitting in her office for fifteen minutes watching the show, I got up escorted a man holding an arm full of folders out of the office and before closing the door I gave Tom instructions not to open the door until I was done. He smiled and stepped in front of the door. I closed it and took my seat.

"For someone who just lost her boss you don't look very concerned, Ms. Ronson." I never broke eye contact.

"Mr. Calhoun for your information this company will not run itself. I have a Board of Directors I must answer to which you made painfully clear during your phone call two days ago."

I fixed a steely gaze upon her. Delilah Ronson was a very striking women, a bit older than I was, jet-black hair pulled back in a conservative bun, coal black eyes that looked very deep, and a chin that appeared to be chiseled from granite.

There was a familiarity about her but I couldn't quite put my finger on it. She was well proportioned, a bit on the thin side for my taste. She sat across from me behind an opulent mahogany desk,

162

opened a marble box, reached in and extracted a long thin cigarette. She placed it in an equally long ebony holder, clenched it in her teeth, I offered her a light, she instead hefted a matching marble decorative lighter with little effort from her desk and struck a flame. As she exhaled smoke rings wafted across the desk from me. She placed the lighter back on the desk without making a sound, the muscles in her forearm were now the most impressive feature about her.

"Well, I have a job to do and it includes your full cooperation." She came around her desk and sat in an adjoining wingback. She crossed her legs, adjusting her skirt and peered into my eyes. "You have my undivided attention, for ten minutes."

"I'm assigning you a bodyguard. She will go everywhere you go. My men are in the middle of performing a threat assessment and are making adjustments to the already existing security system." I took a deep breath and continued, "We also took the liberty of posting a roving security patrol and are searching all the containers on the grounds for any weapons or explosive devices as we speak."

She never even raised an eyebrow. That surprised me. Usually the protectee puts up some type of a fight. They will argue that having someone on them 24-7 is invading and makes their life difficult. Or they are afraid of what their peers might think. Or even that the person protecting them will attack the protectee's significant other without knowing it. Everything I've mentioned here is quite possible. I've been on the job before and see the bodyguard stereotype and attack the protectee's significant other all in the name of protecting his client.

A trained professional will not make this mistake. Because during the interview process, during which time the professional protection agent interviews the client, not the other way around, he/she will glean this information and write it down in the personal profile which should also include pictures if at all possible.

It's the little things that make the difference between a good bodyguard and an excellent protection agent.

"Will that be all Mr. Calhoun?" she looked put out and unimpressed. I keyed my lapel mike and let out a slight hiss. The door opened and Bina entered. Tom shut the door behind her. I introduced the women to each other and stood back. It was like watching two dogs sniffing around each other in a park. They looked each other up and down, circled each other three times and moved to neutral corners.

"Mr. Calhoun, don't you think because I'm female it would be awkward to be seen with a female." I smirked, the first objection. "I'm sorry, I forgot to inform you, from now on you will clear your personal itinerary with me."

I winked at her and told her I got that approval directly from the board. If I am not available, you will clear it with the assistant team leader, are we clear?" "Crystal." This is too easy I thought to myself. She is giving in way too easy. "Will that be all?"

I winked at Bina on the way out. She mimed a kiss with a sarcastic tone. I left the girls to get acquainted. Tom raised an eyebrow at me as I went past him. I frowned and shrugged my shoulders; I'm not in the mood. He smiled and made the okay sign with his fingers.

By the time I returned to the impromptu office we were set up in, bosons mate third class Pepper Calhoun had informed me he had the place wired. "The thang about it is, you would think that being on the cutting edge of technology they would have a state of the art phone system." I lifted an eyebrow. "But they don't." I sat across from him at a conference table that would comfortably seat 20 people as he laid it all out.

"I hard wired the system at the junction box which is just down the hall next to the janitor's closet. You're gonna love this, in fact the wall separating the two rooms doesn't even go all the way to the ceiling. You have access to it without getting too much attention. Early this morning I went into town with Roger and I bought a new palmtop PC. It has a modem in it. I wired that into the VPOTC's phone line. I have that set to forward any faxes or email into your box." He was so pleased with himself and he let everyone know it.

"Damn P you have been keeping busy haven't you?"

"Just trying to earn my keep Big Brother."

Toshio meanwhile had the Human Resources guy install a computer in our office so we would have direct and up to date information on schedules, meetings, and our very own e-mail address. According to the HR guy, who's name we stopped trying to figure out, we were to check our box at least every half hour for any changes that would be made at the last minute as far as travel outside the plant was concerned.

For the first three days nothing happened. We enforced new security policies, we searched all vehicles as they entered and exited the grounds, and after working very closely with the existing security staff, in three days do you know what we found? Nothing. Not a goddamn thing. I was beginning to think the company was being paranoid.

At approximately 1900 hours Thursday Tom took the roving sentry patrol of the parking and loading docks. He reported in at twenty-minute intervals. At approximately 2015 hours, he reported that he was going to check on some noise he heard on the far side of the loading docks. During the exchange Roger informed us there were no scheduled loads at this time. PQ and MC started to back Tom up from their location, but announced over the radio it would take them three minutes to get there. Tom switched his microphone to full VOX (Voice Operated Control). That way we could hear him and any conversation and he could keep his hands free and not alert anyone to the fact that we were listening. He whispered into the boom mike that he could see five men moving about near an open container. MC and PQ informed us they were about two minutes out and closing. Tom said he was moving in for a closer look. What follows is the exchange between him and the suspects.

We heard him call out, "Can I help you guys?"

"We're one out" Puffed PQ into his mike.

"Holy shit, I thought you were..." the sound we heard was unmistakable. Four silenced rounds fired at close range. We could hear men in the distance over Tom's radio calling out.

"Let's go, let's go, and hurry up goddammit." The rest of the team scrambled to their positions. I ran to the VPOTC's office and burst through the door. Bina had her cowering in the corner, while she stood in front of her. I am positive she shit herself. I closed and locked the door. While Roger was covering the other two VP's and securing them in another office, I left and ran down the front stairs, out past the lobby and into the front parking area. I was just in time to watch one tractor-trailer and one sedan exiting through the gate. Machine gun fire riddled the guard shack. I emptied my 45 into the back of the sedan. In a blink of an eye they were gone.

By the time MC found Tom he was dead. Pepper spent the next twenty minutes with several of the plant's security guards going through the rest of the building. PQ called for the helicopter to do an extraction. Roger and Bina brought the VPOTC and the rest of the VP's to the waiting chopper. Roger put Bina and the employees inside and sent them to the hotel. He gave Bina instructions for her to wait there.

Pepper took one of the cars and drove over to the hotel. I instructed them all to wait for us to get back. It was shaping up to be a long night. After everybody had been sent off, I met Roger at the loading dock. Roger was busy securing the crime scene.

As I approached the tape border, one of the Japanese security guards lifted it. I nodded at him and ducked underneath, joining Roger. "What's wrong with this picture?" Roger had a sour look on his face. I stood over Tom's lifeless body and surveyed the scene.

"The first thing I noticed was there were no spent shells." Roger nodded, "Keep going". "Tom's radio is gone." "Uh-huh, what else?" I knelt down; Tom had something clenched in his hand.

"Should we bag this?" Roger looked at me and shook his head from side to side. I peeled Tom's fingers open and extracted a small piece of paper. It appeared it had been ripped off a larger piece. MC shined his Sure Fire light on it. "It looks like money, yen maybe."

The paper was crisp like a new bill. Roger bent down and started searching through Tom's pockets. Except for the keys to one of the cars there was nothing there, nothing, no money, American or otherwise. I find it hard to believe he was mugged. I looked at MC and PQ, "Any ideas?"

They both shrugged their shoulders. I stood up and began to rub the torn piece of paper in my right hand. I looked down on the ever-expanding pool of blood and took one step back.

I looked around. PQ was already fanning out with the rest of the team searching for clues. After spending three hours methodically going over the parking lot bit by bit, section by section, we didn't have shit. If evidence was leather, we couldn't saddle a flea. Fuck me running, again.

Roger was finally able to get Bina on the phone at the VPOTC's condo. She had nothing to add or report. By the time I got done with the local police and got underway to the hotel it was after midnight. Thankfully Pepper had ordered me dinner and kept it warm on the stove. Noodles and rice, anything would've tasted good right about them.

Pepper and Roger let me sleep in. They didn't wake me until 0600, thanks guys. They got me moving and choc full of coffee. We debriefed on the way to the plant. "The cops have less info than we do. Considering the only evidence is the paper and I ain't sharing with them."

It took us 58 minutes to get to the plant. A whopping 12 miles from where we are staying and you think the traffic in LA is bad? I checked my mailbox and sent Janet the latest information. I promised to call her that evening at 1900 hours adjusting for the time difference, which is plus 17 hours. That makes it 1200 hours on the following day. I figured even if I am at the plant, it should be easy to find the time to call her and the kids.

After the morning's meeting concluded, Toshio found me wandering the halls. "Gomen na sai Rowdy-San, may I have a moment of your time?" "Ohio guz, sai mas, Toshio-San, hai." I bowed. "Ahhh, Rowdy you are always so polite to me. How come you never tell me to go fuck myself, as you do your comrades?" I was somewhat stunned. I continued walking. "Toshio, why would you ask me such a thing?" "I have seen you and your team work so closely together. I have overheard some of the comments you make to each other…I have known you for 4 years and you never speak to me this way."

Shit Tosh, if I didn't know any better I would think you are jealous." "In a way I am. We Japanese work together as one toward a common goal, zero defects. We spend more time here at work than with our own families and yet there is no camaraderie." "Well Tosh, if it makes you feel any better, do me a favor and eat shit and bark at the moon." He stood there for a brief moment then let out a loud bark. He slapped me on the back and we continued on.

"Toshio, you didn't ask me out on this private stroll to ask me to curse you, now what's up?" I stopped mid stride and turned to face him. He looked at the ground and started to gently shake his head. "I am ashamed to ask this of you Rowdy-San, however, I have no one else to turn to." I joined him in his glance of the tile floor.

"What can I do for you Toshio-San?" I bowed gently. The sudden quiet conveyed the seriousness of the situation.

"I must ask you to stop investigating Thomas-San's death." I raised an eyebrow. I took a deep breath and spent the next several minutes taking the customary Japanese thinking time. Outwardly it appeared that I was actually mulling it over. The more time I took to give Toshio an answer the more it would look like I was doing him a great service, which would also include him being forever in my debt. Just when I was ready to respond I looked at him looking at the floor and gave him the answer he wanted to hear. By allowing me to take my time I was able to save face in his book. This would make me an honorable man and, let's face it, there was no way in hell I would stop investigating Tom's murder and Toshio knew it. He wanted to be able to tell the Board that our team would back off and let the Tokyo Police do their job.

I went back to our office and like a good little boy, I sent off a memo advising anyone who had e-mail that they were not to talk to anyone on the team about the incident in the loading area. I pulled the team from their assigned duties for an emergency meeting behind closed doors. Pepper and Roger closed the blinds. I was standing in front of the whiteboard which hung from the wall with a red marker in my hand. The pen squeaked across the board as I wrote, "From this moment on any part of our ongoing investigation must be done as clandestinely as possible. If you are caught gathering information, you will suffer the consequences of my public humiliation of you". I turned to look at my team. They looked unhappy. I continued scribbling on the board, "Any information must be brought to my attention in private and not discussed over the radio or in front of anyone".

I turned to face them once again. I explained that the Japanese have a very different way of doing business and that we would make every effort to accommodate them, I winked. They smiled and nodded in agreement. The meeting was dismissed and everyone went back to their assigned posts, everyone except Pepper.

Hey Rowdy, can you help me with something I have in the car?" He rolled his eyes and pointed his head towards the door. "Sure I can, c'mon I've got the time right now." We jogged down the stairs and headed outside toward the car. Pepper was setting a fairly quick pace. "Where's the fire?" He looked distressed. The last time I saw that look was back when he was threatened with being sent to the Ice Station.

"We have a serious problem, but not until we get in the car." "Ok." He tossed me the keys to his car. "You drive!" He seemed pretty excited. I got behind the wheel and drove around the back of the plant parking us out of sight next to a tractor-trailer. "What is so important?"

He pulled a small digital audio transport machine out of his inside breast pocket. "Remember I told you I was able to get into the phone box and computer system?" "Yes." "Well, I was finally able to get this edited." "And?" I shifted in my seat, rolled down the window a bit and lit a cigarette. He pushed play. There was no mistaking it was a very stoic Ms. Ronson talking to a voice I hadn't heard since Mexico.

"WTF?" Pepper played the conversation through. I listened intently about plans for distribution, evacuation and recovering the money for the product, but nothing specific.

"how does the Ronson know Allbright?" Pepper shrugged his shoulders. "Fuck, fuck, fuck!!!" I pounded on the steering wheel. Suddenly I had a bad feeling come over me. "Where is SHE!?" I searched myself for the itinerary. "Shit, I left it upstairs. Get Bina on the radio. Don't say a word, just get them back here ASAP. Never mind. We'll go to her." I drove around the back, picked up MC and continued to the front. I parked the car directly in front of the glass double doors leading into the marble tiled foyer and raced past the receptionist up to the top of the stairs, down the hall to the meeting room. PQ heard me coming before he saw me and met me in the hall.

"What the hell is going on?" "I'll explain in the car, let's go." We raced back down the hall, leapt down the two flights of stairs taking them four at a time and hit the marble at a full gallop.

"Have you found her?" MC was behind the wheel. Pepper put a closed fist in the air. I shut up and listened as MC drove out the front gate and sped through town. While Pepper was talking in code to Bina, I briefed PQ quietly in the backseat. I reached between us and pulled down the armrest to expose the hidden cache of weapons we brought with us. I handed one of the MP5's to MC and one to Pepper.

I pulled out a few more magazines for the weapons and distributed them. I slid the custom built Remington 870 that Scattergun Technologies had made for us. It was full of all sorts of nice features, ghost ring night sights, extended magazine tube, sidesaddle ammo carrier, synthetic stock with a pistol grip and skeltonized butstock capable of being knocked down to accommodate close quarter combat. Such as we were experience rather shortly.

As we rounded the last corner putting us directly across from Bina and the VPOTC, all hell broke loose. I was half out of the car yelling at Bina to get down when two dark colored Toyota sedans parked at the curb belched out their occupants and they simultaneously started firing at us and Bina. The four men dressed in black tactical gear and wear Balaclavas fired slowly and methodically, taking care not to waste ammo.

I dove behind the car, put my ear mike back in and radioed Bina. Nothing. I call MC and got a tsk tsk. I called PQ, another round of tsking. I called Pepper, nothing. I called Pepper again and still nothing. All the while we were pinned down by the automatic machine gun fire.

I took into account Pepper and Bina may be down; I took into account we were pinned down but in a good tactical position; I took into account this was probably a setup from the word go and I walked us into it. Well, fuck me running again. Roger called us on the radio wanting real time intel. I put MC in charge of that. I had a problem to deal with. Richard Allbright had once told me if you have a large problem and you meet it head on chances are you will come out okay.

I double checked my Glock 21. All 16 rounds present and accounted for. I re holstered. I racked the slide on my 870 sending the first of an alternating double odd buck, rifled Sabot round combination into the chamber. I had 8 rounds total. I winked at PQ and rolled left out from behind the car and came up firing. For a change things seemed to be going my way. The 2 dick heads closest to me were reloading.

Too late, so solly cholly. I hit them hard and fast. The first caught the buckshot mid chest and in the face. The second one fielded my sabot round in the region of his belt buckle; most of his ass was scattered all over the car behind him. I blindly fired my next two rounds in the general direction of where I remember the other two fuck stains were, shit where'd they go?

I quickly glanced around and saw Pepper and MC, smoke pouring out of their guns. Two more bad guys lay dead on the street. I ran across the now vacant street and leapt over the trunk of one of the Toyota's, landing on the sidewalk. I could see Bina laying across Delilah. She had pushed them up close against one of the many street cart vendors to provide cover. I rushed to her side and turned her over.

She had no pulse. Her pupils were fixed and dilated. As I sat there in the filthy gutter half way around the world, I began to think at warp speed. Ponce was kneeling next to me and informed me that the Delilah and the rest of the team was ready to move out. I cradled Bina's body as PQ helped me get to my feet. I carried her to one of the Toyota's MC had appropriated, gently laid Bina across the backseat and told PQ to give me a second.

I could hear the Hi-Lo sirens wailing, getting ever closer. I ran back across the street and peeled off the black hood on the closest asshole to me. Caucasian. I rummaged through his pockets. No wallet, only about 500 yen. PQ called me over to the body of the guy with no cock. "Look at this." He had found a small piece of paper in the breast pocket. "Look, or should I say, feel familiar?" he asked.

By now the cops were within a block or two. "C'mon you two, we gotta go." MC whispered into the mike. PQ and I sprang up and darted to the car. Ponce slid behind the wheel and I got in the back with Bina. First I called Roger on the cell phone and gave him a heads up. He told us to go directly to the hotel and he would meet us there later. Second I ordered MC to find an alley suitable for an interrogation. He did and we pulled in behind him.

Delilah demanded to know what was going on, so did I. I ripped her door open and grabbed her by the arm yanking her out of the backseat. I pulled her around at breakneck speed throwing her up against the rear fender and pushing her face down on the trunk. I pushed her skirt up around her waist. "Here's the deal you fucking cunt. You tell me what is going on or so help me we are going to run a train on you with such force Amtrak will be jealous."

MC grabbed her arms and stretched them tight across the trunk. She was on her tiptoes now, her tight ass swinging in the breeze. I slipped my Emerson under the rose colored thong that kept her from being totally exposed. She flinched as the cold steel came in contact with her smooth backside.

I leaned in closer, "If you don't tell me what I want to know, by the time we are done with you you'll be able to park your BMW in that tight little ass of yours" I hissed. I cut the thong between the waistband and her pussy, kicked her legs apart and reached between them pulling the material away exposing her to the world. She lasted longer than I thought she would but she finally began to spill her guts.

The alarm went off on my watch reminding me it was time to call Janet. I told MC to take notes while I was gone. He nodded and I climbed into the backseat of the car.

Janet was telling me about a hijacking that was on TV. She relayed the information as we talked. A tractor-trailer was stolen from the dock in Long Beach. This particular trailer happened to be full of parts from this plant and coincidentally I asked Janet if she could see any marking on the trailer. She rattled off a few numbers. Bingo! Same numbers as on the truck that left the night Tom was killed.

Janet got off the subject and was telling me about how she finished her class on the new food stamp ATM cards that everyone is changing over to. "Everyone?" I asked. "Yes. The Feds are getting rid of the paper money, they say it's too hard to track and it produces too much waste." "What do you mean too much waste?" "After the clients use them in the store, the store owner accounts for them and then he sends them to be traded back to him in the form of cash." "Uh huh. What do they do with the stamps after that?" I had all kinds of bells and whistles going off in my head. "They burn it, I think." "Janet, do me a favor. Send me samples of this money overnight express." "Okay handsome, I'll send it out tomorrow." I snapped back, "No. Tomorrow will be too late. I need it tomorrow." "Is there something wrong? I mean is everything okay?" I wavered, "Yeah, everything is fine", I said as I looked out the back window at the Delilah who was naked from the waist down and had a bunch of horny pissed off Spec warriors standing around just thinking of the prospect of doing this chick just for shits and giggles. Now I know what your thinking, whoa Rowdy, since when do you stoop to rape? Well, actually I never would nor would any of the guys but she doesn't know that, and I figure after losing two friends in two days, what she doesn't know won't hurt her.

"Honey?" "Sorry, I was distracted for a sec, we're driving downtown." "Can I say hi to Pepper?" This was a test. She was making sure he wasn't far and even more so making sure he wasn't hurt or dead. "Hang on a sec. Pep! It's for you." "Hi from Pepper!" he said half giggling. "Hi honey, how's things?" "Everything here is under control", he winked at me. "Okay, give me back to Rowdy. I love you!" "Love you too, here he is." He handed me the phone. "So can ya send me that stuff today, please?!" "Yes, I'll go as soon as I hang up." "Thanks. You have no idea what it means to me. Well I gotta go. We have been sitting in an alley for a few minutes now trying to keep a clear signal. I love you." "I love you too. We all miss you." "I miss you guys too."

I pressed the end key and disconnected the call. I lit a cigarette and got out of the car. "What did I miss?" I ran my hand across her baby smooth butt and gave it a smack. PQ had to turn around to keep from laughing out loud. MC explained the story. It seems our Miss. Brooks here was contacted by Allbright and threatened into submission pretty much the same way we just did. He smiled. As luck would have it the company ships directly into a U.S. Customs Port and because they supply the Government with their computer smart chips they never get inspected. They are guarded and then

174

transferred to a container and driven directly to a secure location to be installed in computers used by all those 3 letter agencies.

In case you haven't figured it out yet, the perfect smuggling and counterfeiting operation starts right here at the plant with the help of the Ms. Ronson. Allbright is counterfeiting food stamps outside the U.S., hence nothing for the Feds to trace. Allbright kidnaps the POTC of a company outside the U.S., preferably Japanese because the Japanese regard their employees as a family and will pay any price to get them back alive, including allowing themselves to be used as a smuggling operation to guarantee the safe return of their employee. However, the first attempt was botched. The Tokyo Police found a POTC inside an abandoned warehouse on the outskirts of town.

Allbright strikes again. He kidnaps our POTC, holds him for ransom until he gets his counterfeit food stamps across the ocean and distributed, then he collects a ransom fee from the corporation and disappears. Before the Government even realizes what happened, the money he has flooded the market with is burned and there is no trace. SNAFU, Situation Normal, All Fucked Up.

It all makes perfect sense. The last shipment out was hijacked, the company told me nothing was missing. That led us to believe that something was smuggled out, but what? My first thought was extra chips. I mean they would never be missed. The hijacking looks random. The bad guys steal a truck, open it up and nothing to sell in a back alley in New York off the back of a truck. The only red flag is that when the truck is jacked, four federal guards are killed in the process. Not exactly something the average carjacker attempts. But hey it could happen.

I nodded at Phil. He let her go and she slid off the trunk. I grabbed her by the arm and tossed her back in the car and slammed the door. Pepper looked at me, "What?!" "I can't remember the last time you lost your temper." "The thang about it is" I said doing a Pepper impression "I haven't lost my temper…yet."

Fuck her running.

175

CHAPTER 26
ALLBRIGHT

Delilah Ronson sat in the backseat next to me sniffling. She had her legs crossed in order to keep what little dignity she had left. "Have you contacted Roger yet?" asked PQ as we pulled up in front of the hotel. Nope. Now that we know the whole scoop, I don't want anyone knowing we know, ya' know?" Ponce shook his head in agreement.

I called Roger on the radio from downstairs. He cleared his throat, "C'mon, all clear. Let's get moving!" As we ran from the curb outside the hotel, PQ tossed his keys at the Valet, "Park this in a good spot. All this happened the last time I was here," he said referring to the several shotgun blasts and blood splatter marks on the side of the car.

We hightailed it toward the elevators and at the last minute I paused. I steered everyone into the stairwell. I figured that at least inside the stairwell we have a fighting chance if someone is waiting for us. MC took point, PQ took the rear and here I am stuck in the middle with Pepper and Ronson. By the time we got to the 25th floor we were all drenched. Stress is a motherfucker. I handed Ronson over to MC and motioned Roger to come with me into a private room so I could brief him.

"You've got to be kidding me." The look on Roger's face pretty much said it all. If he wasn't here to see it all he wouldn't believe a word of it. Pepper brought me the Sat-phone. I punched in the number the company boys gave me and after 12 or so rings a gruff voice answered. "What?" "Lt. Commander R. Calhoun reporting."

"Hold please Commander."

"Commander Calhoun, how's things in Japan?" it was the older guy with the pipe

"We have an identifiable, verifiable threat." His tone changed.

"Is this a secure line?"

"Yes sir."

"Go on."

"We have reason to believe the government shipment that was hijacked yesterday was the work of Richard Allbright."

"Hmm, I see, and you have proof of this I take it?"

"Yes. I have the confession of the VP Delilah Ronson as to the how's and why's. She admitted to having contact with Allbright and to agreeing to let him use the company as a cover to smuggle counterfeit food stamps within the container trucks bound for the U.S." I heard him clear his throat then cover the mouthpiece. I could also hear a muffled voice in the background.

"And I suppose she gave you this information freely and of her own will?" I thought to myself, who gives a shit as long as she admitted to it.

"Affirmative" I lied. Sue me. "Hmm" more muffled voices.

"Do you have a sworn statement given to the proper authorities?"

"Huh?"

"Have you turned her over to the police?"

"Negative."

"So she is in your custody?"

"Affirmative."

"Where are you now?"

"Hang on a sec. I'll ask the driver." I motioned Roger to me. He leaned in close; "He wants to know where we are." Roger took his index finger and drew it slowly across his throat.

"We are on the South side of Tokyo, looking for a new hotel."

"Give me 20 minutes, we will have someone meet you and take the woman."

"You know where to reach me." I clicked off.

Roger was already packing his bags and suggested we do the same. We did as we were advised. MC handcuffed the woman to a shower bar in the bathroom so we could have a POW wow. Roger spoke first. "We have about 15 minutes left in this hotel and then we must be gone. It is going to be very hard to exit the country now. I'm sure the company has already notified customs and our pictures are being printed on milk cartons as we speak."

I took the floor. "Roger is right. We now have to fall back on being and doing what we trained to do three and a half years ago in San Diego. Teamwork is going to be essential. I am just as upset as you are for the loss of Tom and Bina. However, we need to focus here and now if we ever expect to leave this country on our own accord." The phone rang in the bedroom. I took a chance.

"Mushi Mushi."

"Rowdy, it's Face. Meet me at the airfield in 45 minutes. I have the TFB plane. We can leave as soon as you get there, if I was you I would keep a low profile."

The phone went dead. Now for those that haven't been paying close attention. Face got on the plane with us at Brown Field, but never got off in Tokyo. He has been our ace in the hole this entire trip. He has been following us around, looking over our shoulders, just generally being there in case we needed him. And man did we need him right now.

The team had assembled in the hall with all our gear. MC had the Veep. We were indeed ready to travel. Pepper and PQ went down the hall first. Roger and Delilah in the middle and MC and I brought up the rear. Unfortunately, we nixed the idea of the stairwell, too much gear and a woman who had no desire to go with us. Hence she put up a struggle every step of the way.

We opted instead for the service elevators and headed down to the 12th floor first. We got off there and waited a few minutes. We summoned the elevator again and took an offensive stance as it approached our floor. The doors opened and hell followed. We were ready, they were not. It was a blood bath. The four guys in golf attire had a hard time reaching their weapons in the golf bags before we obliterated them and everything else in the elevator. After the smoke cleared we drug them out and got in.

"Don't lean against the walls. That blouse might get something on it" PQ said referring to the grey matter that clung to the interior walls like a tick on an old hound dog.

She couldn't hold it back any longer and started gagging like it was the end of prom night. "You owe me twenty bucks" PQ grinned as MC pulled a twenty out of his pants pocket and handed it to him.

MC looked at me, smile coyly and said, "It was worth it."

I stood there shaking my head "I just shined these boots".

We exited the elevator slowly. Nothing. "C'mon, the coast is clear." MC motioned us to the cars. He had already pilfered two sets of keys from the Valet box. We were on our way. Hopefully the guests wouldn't be going anywhere for a while. We sped out and mingled with the early afternoon traffic. It only took us 22 minutes to get to the airport. That has to be a new record. We abandoned the cars at the curb and locked them, taking the keys, MC called in a bomb threat just to make sure all attention would not be on us. That should keep the police uptight and busy for a little while.

We threaded our way towards the private gated area. The guard booth had only two people in it; one had his back to us. I could see the TFB plane taxiing out of the garage area. I asked the guard for a light in Japanese. As he reached into his pants pocket I slugged him. His partner jumped up but before he could react, MC cold cocked him and he dropped like a sack of rice. Pepper reached in and opened the gate. We strutted through like we owned the place. I motioned everybody past me and closed the gate.

Face was on the radio; "You guys coming or what?" "On our way" Roger answered. PQ turned to me "What do you want to do with the girl?" "We don't need to add international kidnapping to the growing list of charges." I smiled.

I grabbed Delilah by the three links in between the cuffs, reached into my pocket and pulled out the key. "You should keep low until we deal with Allbright. He may come back thinking you gave him up." She nodded. I looked into her eyes. She bore no emotion on her face.

"Mr. Calhoun…thank you." She turned to leave. I still had her by the one cuff I hadn't removed. "I have to do this, sorry." I cuffed her to the fence and jogged to the plane. Everyone else was already on board.

Roger had set up the Sat-phone, fax machine and e-mail. We were in business. The first call I made was to Toshio. I had to let him know so he could report to the Board. He explained that the Board would quietly make her disappear. He asked if I and the rest of the team were okay and said he would see to it personally all the arrangements to getting Bina and Tom home. He also assured me he would smooth over our past indiscretions with the police. We exchanged our good-byes and I clicked off.

The second call I made was to let my good friend David know his sister was dead. It's times like these that I hate this job. But I didn't want to put off the inevitable. The call with David lasted just under 40 minutes and he said he would meet us in California at the airport. He was finishing up a protective detail at the Israeli Consulate in Los Angeles and had a few days of R&R coming to him.

I called the company guys again to ask them if they were going to help with this situation. As far as they were concerned there was no reason to. There was nothing stolen from them, therefore, as we say in law enforcement, "no victim, no crime". They had already held a news conference telling the world that the hijacked shipment was part of an anti-terrorist exercise. Nothing was stolen thereby creating a window of opportunity as far as national security is concerned. The good guys can show how nothing gets by them and the world gets a good impression of our government hard at work stopping terrorism. Yeah right.

What about the guards that were killed in the attack you ask? Nonsense. The nice people from the National Security Counsel got right up in front of all those news people and said it never happened. Why on earth would they lie? Oh my! Because the guards signed a clause in their contract that signs away any rights as far as injury or death is concerned. And just to make sure a really nice man in a dark suit doesn't show up at the homes of the guards and visits with their widows and kids explaining that if they go public, their insurance money and widows slush fund would dry up and disappear. Welcome to bureaucracy at it's finest.

After my call to the idiots, we were now considered PNG that's Persona Non Grata. Don't feel bad, I had to ask too. I asked Pepper to get Roger and give us a few minutes alone. "I can't help but think I let the team down Roger." "I don't think they feel that way at all." He drummed his fingers on the table.

"I'm glad you think so, but after Tom and Bina…I don't know what to think anymore." "Rowdy, don't kick yourself until it is completely over. We still have to deal with Richard, a man's life still hangs in the balance." He was of course referring to the POTC. As far as we knew he was still alive.

"By the way, this came by messenger just before you guys got to the hotel." He handed me a Fed Ex package. I ripped it open. I slowly started chewing a hole through my lower lip.

"Were you correct in your deduction?" "It looks like a perfect match to me." I handed Roger the samples of the food stamps Janet sent along with the original piece Tom left for us to find.

"I think you hit it right on the head with this one. Very good work." It was good to be recognized by Roger for this development. I still remember him telling me to use my rank wisely and do the best I could for my fellow teammates. I was hoping I was doing both.

I got up to stretch my legs. Pepper was sitting in front of the computer terminal constantly checking for anything from anybody about anything. "Nothing yet." I walked past him to the cockpit.

"Hey Face, thanks for being there."

"Shit, your not gonna get all mushy on me are ya'?" he laughed.

"I don't wanna start crying. It'll fog up the windshield." I squeezed his shoulder. He nodded. I closed the cabin door behind me. I flopped into one of the recliners and closed my eyes. The Sat-phone rang. MC was closest.

"Yes, I see. Uh huh. I will let him know. Thank you."

We all looked at him. "That was Toshio. He said they found the girl at the airport and she is being dealt with, but that ain't the best part...It seems that Ms. Ronson has confessed to being Allbright's illegitimate daughter. He also said that the rest of the team is on their way home."

"At least we know why she did it huh?" Pepper grumbled

I breathed a sigh of relief. The one thing that was drilled into me enough was no one gets left behind. I didn't want to start making a new tradition now. Face made the announcement over the PA that we would be landing in Hawaii in about a half an hour. According to him it would take about 30 minutes to refuel and get back under way. I figured about 45 minutes total. We made good time, about 4 hours and 15 minutes with a tail wind.

"Roger, who do you know here that can get some Intel on what's going on?" He looked at me, smiled and got on the phone. The next twenty minutes after we landed we were having a fun-filled romp through the Navy's Intelligence Department.

Roger's friend Stan gave us free run of the place. Pepper was connected on-line in fifteen seconds downloading all sorts of really useful stuff. I got on the radio and had Ponce clean up the Scattergun Technologies shotgun. What the hell. It was proven in battle and it seemed like the perfect early Christmas gift. I gave Roger the aluminum lockbox. He gave me the thumbs up sign and headed into the XO's office. I could hear him from outside. He sounded pretty happy.

Face radioed we were ready to go. I told him we needed another half-hour. As Roger and I drove back to the airport he told me Allbright was asking for favors nobody wanted to grant. "It seems that even though you are PNG, the brass wants to see how you will handle this. So no one wants to get in bed with Richard. Their gonna let you play this hand out."

"Great."

My problem was I had no idea where Richard was. What his plan might be and where he may be headed after he followed through with it. I leaned back in my seat and enjoyed the view trying to clear my head for a few minutes.

My cell phone rang. "Yeah."

"You guys need to get back the plane, now."

"We're about 5 out. What's up?"

"Allbright sent a fax and e-mail." I motioned for Roger to pick up the pace.

"Tell Face I want the jet hot and ready to lift off as soon as we get there."

"Sir, yes sir." He clicked off.

"Allbright sent us a message." Roger rolled his eyes; "here we go again."

MC pulled the retractable steps up behind us and Face was already moving. He came over the PA, "Gentlemen, please make sure tray tables are up and your seats are in the upright and locked position." We were in the air before you could say buckle up.

"Allbright wants you to meet him to exchange the POTC for the money." I pointed to myself and raised my eyebrows.

"Uh huh. You big guy." Pepper sat down next to me and whispered in my ear, "I don't like it. You know he wants you dead."

"Ponce!"

"Sir?"

"You are the best man I know for logistics. What is going on and what are our chances of outflanking him?"

Ponce already had all the maps out. He was trying to get a fix on what Allbright wanted. It wasn't looking good. He shifted some of the topographical maps around and laid down a grid giving us ten square miles to work with.

"He wants to meet you here"; he drew a circle in red grease pencil. I knew the area well. So did Pepper. The dry lake bed in the high desert near Hesperia, California.

"Shit, he can see for miles out there." Pepper was not happy at the prospect of offering his brother up as a sacrificial lamb to Allbright.

"This is fucked. You save me from going to the Arctic so I can watch you get killed right here in our own backyard?"

"Calm down, nobody's gonna kill me, right?" I nervously scanned the team.

"Not if we can help it" chimed MC.

"Holy shit". I jumped up like somebody kicked me and started dancing around the plane.

"WTF?" The guys must have thought I was losing it.

"Pepper, what is this weekend? Think." His face lit up and was taken over by a huge smile.

"Would you two like to fill us in?" Roger crossed his arms across his chest. In stereo we answered him, "Thanksgiving weekend."

"So the fuck what?"

"The thing about it is, everybody goes to the desert this weekend with their off-road toys, quads, dune buggy's, sand rails, motorcycles, you name it, it's out there. It can't get any better than this." PQ grinned.

"This could work out to our benefit."

"Hey guys, 45 minutes from Ontario International."

"The latest from Richard has us meeting him at high noon near this area right here." Ponce explained we would need a GPS and he was working on getting everyone as close to the site as possible.

"Pepper, we need to send someone by my house. Janet doesn't answer the phone."

"Ruh roh, my bad. I sent her e-mail and told her to meet Sharon and go to a hotel."

"Thanks Pep." He winked at me.

We landed at Ontario sans fanfare. We rented two cars at Avis and drove over to the Red Roof Inn next door to the airport. We checked in and got cleaned up and headed for the Jacuzzi for a half hour. When we got back to the rooms I had laid out all of the weapons and had started to clean them, separated the ammo and figured out who would carry what and where everyone would be.

Pepper stuck his nose in the air, took a big sniff and declared there was a gun shop nearby. "I'll be back." He sounded like the Terminator.

MC and Roger were passed out on the bed. Through the door that adjoined the two rooms I could see Ponce sprawled across his bed. Not a creature was stirring, except me of course. I picked up the cell phone and paged Janet. A few minutes later she called back.

"Welcome home. Will you be staying long?"

"Hi honey, how is everyone?" I asked ignoring her painfully obvious shitty remark.

"Can you tell me where you are at least?"

"I'm in Ontario. We still have some business to conclude."

"I see. Any idea when you will be home?"

"If all goes well, I should be home in a couple of days." I gritted my teeth. I had all the intentions of not lying to her, SFSG. I could tell she was thoroughly disgusted with me, so I shortened the conversation and hung up, claiming I had another call.

Pepper walked in at the same time the Sat-phone rang. I let it ring and after eight it stopped. Then my pager went off. I read the display, it was the company.

"Maybe they want to help". I looked up at P with utter surprise.

"Ok, so maybe I'm an idiot." "Maybe." We smiled at each other.

I fired up the computer to check our mail and lo and behold what do my eyes see? Richard has confirmed the meeting; however, he had added some new rules to the ever-changing game that we were playing. I gathered the team together and went over our options.

"Hey guys, listen up. We got another letter from Allbright detailing tomorrow's meeting." I lit a smoke and tossed the pack to Pepper. It was intercepted by Ponce who snagged one and lit it, passing the pack on to Pep.

I had printed copies of the letter and passed them out. The instructions were simple:

To: Rowdy Calhoun
From: R.A.
Subject: Rules of engagement

Please find the enclosed rules listed below. I expect you as an officer to obey each and every one to the letter.

Any deviation will result in termination of our agreement and your package. You have been a worthy adversary; however, you are out of your league.

I expect full cooperation. Remember you still have an interest in the positive outcome of tomorrow's meeting.

#1 No one other than Rowdy at the meeting site.
#2 If I see anyone other than Rowdy the hostage will be mailed back to TFB in 6 separate pieces.
#3 The money is to be in an aluminum case.
#4 The POTC will be traded after I get the money.

#5 No guns. (For you anyway)
#6 No police, Feds, or company men.
#7 Meet me at 1200 hours.

"Hey, this really cheers me up. How 'bout everyone else?" Ponce wrinkled up his copy and tossed a three pointer into the trash can.

"This is a no shitter guys. I am giving you a direct order. Stay behind and let me face him alone. What part of that don't you understand?"

Face was lying on the bed. He put it into perspective. "Can we get paid before you go?" We all started laughing hard enough to cry. I opened the door and walked out into the hall. I was only outside for a few minutes when Roger and MC joined me.

"You guys are the real thing, I'm just playacting here. That crash course in San Diego didn't prepare me for this shit."

"Yes it did." Roger had a very serious look on his face.

"You must be kidding. I am a bodyguard, not a Navy Seal. Besides all this Lt. Commander crap is just so I could keep tabs on what was going on."

MC, who was standing there quietly, suddenly took a swing at me. I ducked and grabbed his arm as it went by, spinning him and pushing him up against the wall.

"See what we mean?"

"You have to stop second guessing yourself. You are as ready to handle Richard as any of us." MC put his arm around me and gave me a thumbs up, "Hooyah Lt. Commander, Hooyah."

"Promise me after this is all over I can back to being Joe Q. Citizen" I half smiled.

"You know I can't promise that Rowdy." Roger said looking me directly in the eyes.

"A man can dream can't he?"

I went back inside the room and packed up some of my gear I would need for my rendezvous with Senior Allbright. Face and Pepper helped me carry all my shit to the car. "Here. MC gave me this to give to you." Face stuck his handout and held a Detonics .45 caliber handgun.

Nice and compact, accurate only for short distance, but it packs a hell of a wallop. My Glock 21, .45 cal was in my shoulder rig, while a Glock 17, 9MM took up residence in a small of the back holster. I stuck the Detonics in my boot and checked to make sure my Emerson knife was still in my back pocket.

Face gave me the once over, gave me a hug and told me good luck. Pepper was visibly upset, "The thing about it is, we didn't go through hell and high water for you to get yourself killed motherfucker." He threw his arms around me.

"You gotta wait a few minutes. We called a buddy of yours and he sent you a present."

"Aww, you shouldn't have."

We stood around the parking lot for a few minutes until a green Yugo pulled into the lot and drove toward us. A young kid with acne got out and asked for Rowdy.

"That's me. What did I win?" "Chester Gasik sends his best sir."

He handed me an aluminum briefcase. "Be careful when you pull up on the handle." He chuckled, got back in his car and in a cloud of blue smoke and exhaust fumes disappeared.

"You guys thought of everything. Thanks." I laid the case on the hood of the green Plymouth rental car and opened it. We all took a deep breath and gazed upon the beautiful H&K MP5 locked in its cradle. The handle was connected to the firing mechanism, a simple one-handed operation. Pull up on the handle and 30 rounds of Remington Golden Saber in 9MM 147 grain subsonic would spew from the barrel chasing away all but the most violent demons society has to offer.

I closed the case and tossed it on the front seat. I put my ear mike in before I got in the car. "Check, check." "Roger, I read 5 by 5." Face gave me thumbs up as I drove away. I looked in my rear view mirror and P was standing at attention, saluting. I stopped the car, got out, turned on my heels to face him and snapped to attention giving him a salute in return. He lowered his hand and I spun around to get back in the car. I was hoping that it would not be the last time I saw my brother again.

It took three minutes to get to the 15 freeway North heading toward Barstow. The traffic was moderate considering it was a holiday weekend. Lots of motor homes towing trailers of quads, motorcycles and all sorts of desert toys.

As I got closer I thought all those thoughts you think when faced with uncertainty. What do I do if this happens? What if that happens? Blah, blah, blah. After a while I rolled down the window and lit a cigarette. I turned up the radio and let my mind wander. I couldn't help but think about David. I was really looking forward to seeing him. It had been a few years since the last time we got together. I figured it nothing else I could comfort him, assure him his big sister died for a reason and saved the client's life.

I figured if nothing else I could comfort him, assure him his big sister died for a reason and saved the client's life. "Well shit. I'll have to get with him before he returns to Israel." It was all wishful thinking however as my odds with Allbright were nowhere near in my favor and it was a good chance David would be sitting shiva over both of us.

I exited Sidewinder Road and headed west into the desert. I

wasn't alone, besides the holiday revelers, I had been followed since the bottom of Cajon Pass. The driver was pretty good but I was able to pick him out when I got off at Bear Valley Road and got back on by driving along the frontage road until Main Street.

Now I had been able to confirm Allbright wasn't playing by his own rules. What a surprise.

CHAPTER 27
VAYA CON DIOS

The turbulent dust storm being kicked up by my car precluded me from any type of view out the back window. I had no idea if I was being followed anymore and at this point if I stopped I figured anyone tailing me might get upset. The rules of engagement and all.

I kept driving alternating between looking where I was going and looking at the GPS. The coordinates I plugged in before I left the hotel were getting close. I started to slow down. I was not anticipating a showdown in the middle of nowhere. All I wanted was to get the POTC back in one piece. If I had a chance at Richard so be it. I couldn't risk the POTC's life in the process.

The weather was seasonably cold for this time of the year. In the high 60's during the day and dipping near the ice making mark at night. It seemed very warm to me; in fact I was sweating buckets.

I had maintained radio silence in the event Richard was tracking any wavelengths. I didn't want him to know I had an earful of help. I arrived a bit ahead of schedule. I had the feeling Allbright would have me arrive first. This way he is at a tactical advantage. I looked around. There were several large motor homes in close proximity; Allbright and his henchmen could occupy any or all of them. I felt I was under surveillance but by how many was anyone's guess.

After waiting outside the car for an hour and twenty minutes a limo drove out from around one of the larger motor homes and headed right for me. The driver stopped and opened the door to get out. He had a devilish grin on his face. I could see him level a Colt .45 at me.

"Hi ya' Trevor, you still mad at me?"

"Nah, why do ya' ask?"

"I was wondering if you plan on using that iron on me is all."

He smiled at me. "Well, I reckon if I get a chance I might just take it."

"I see. Anything I can say to you to keep that from happening?"
"I don't think so."

"All right. I do appreciate your honesty though."

"Sure thing. Glad I could oblige ya'. By the way, how's Pepper doing?"

"He's good. If he was here I'm sure he'd send his love."

I kept looking around, making sure I didn't lose whatever tactical edge I had left. Trevor looked pretty happy to see me and that was a bad sign. I couldn't wait to see the look on Richard's face.

The cars sat nose to nose with about 12 feet between the bumpers. Trevor had positioned himself between the car door and the inside of the car itself. I was mostly exposed with half of my lower body behind the fender. Trevor knew this and he loved every minute of it. The passenger rear door of the limo opened and almost in slow motion Richard Allbright got out of the car and stood behind the door. I had a sneaky suspicion this vehicle was armored. The only shot I had was a headshot.

Now under normal circumstances I could probably hit him if my gun was already drawn. If was trained on him. If I didn't have to deal with all that flying dust and sand. Too many variables to overcome.

Besides that, Trevor looked like he was waiting for a reason to turn me into coyote pate. I looked at him again. His shit-eating grin was getting bigger by the second.

"Where's the money?" he shouted.

"Go fuck yourself Trevor. I'm here to deal with Richard.

You're just an errand boy." I could see that pissed him off to no end. He raised his gun. Richard shouted at him to stop.

"You must know by now that Richard wants to kill me all by himself. If you pull that trigger he'll kill you, just like he killed your partner in Japan." His jaw dropped, Allbright grinned.

"The way I figure it Richard, your trained monkeys got out of hand and killed the other POTC by mistake, causing you to lose your temper and shoot him eight times. How am I doing so far?"

"Not bad kid, keep going." I smiled back at him.

"Well, what I came up with was, you decided to get even with me. But that was just a bonus after you figured out what it was you were going to counterfeit and smuggle." He nodded.

"So you decided to make your own food stamps knowing full well they can't be traced if no one is paying attention. The stamps hit the street, they get paid off and then they get burned. By the time anyone even has a clue to what or where the stamps came from, they are incinerated. No evidence, no cops. No cops, no trial. No trial, no jail."

"Please get to the point. I have roughly 20 million including the 5 million you have for me, to spend."

"I have it on the front seat, but first I want to see Mr. Akimura." He waved a bony finger at me.

"Not until you throw your hardware on the ground…all of it." I reached into my jacket and Trevor jumped, extending his gun as far away from his body as possible.

"One false move shit head and I will drill you." I slowly pulled my .45 out and tossed it away. "Now the other one." I reached around my right side and pulled the 9MM out of its holster and tossed it also. "Okay, now take off your jacket and turn around very slowly." I complied.

"When do I see Akimura?" I shouted. Allbright reached into the car and yanked the Asian out by his hair.

"The money!" I opened the driver's door and leaned in across the console. I grabbed the case and at the same time I lifted my right leg up and pulled the Detonics .45 out of my boot. I concealed the little gun in the palm of my hand. I stood up and took a look around. I slammed the car door and walked toward the front of the car.

"What are our chances for getting out of this alive?" I asked rather casually. Allbright and Trevor looked at each other for a brief second.

"Chances? You want chances? How about being left for dead in an alley behind a restaurant, with most of my throat torn out. What were my chances for survival?"

"You are a wife beater you piece of shit. If you were stuck on my shoe I would scrape you off before I got in my car. You're pathetic. Beating up on Ruth and the kids. You fuck!"

"If you would have taken a bullet that night in the alley it wouldn't have had to come to this Rowdy."

"Trevor you scumbag. I can't wait to kill you. The Chief was my friend, your father-in-law, and Ruth's dad. Shit you have no redeeming qualities. It will be my pleasure to watch you die!"

Trevor brought his Colt up and in an instant he vaporized into a red mist. There were pieces of him everywhere.

"Shiiiiit!!!!" I banked right over the hood of the Plymouth, the briefcase still in my hand. I landed on the ground next to where most of Trevor had been blown to.

"Richard?"

"Rowdy god dammit. I told you to come alone!"

"Fuck you asshole. I did come alone!" My heart was ready to burst through my chest.

"Then what was that?"

"Hang on I'll call the psychic hotline."

"Are you still willing to deal?"

"Give me the money and you can have the Jap."

"Sounds like a plan."

"I'll tell you what. On the count of three, stand up and we'll start over."

"Sure Dick, anything you say."

"One!" I had the Detonics .45 in one hand and the briefcase full of attitude in the other. "Two!" I closed my eyes and tried to focus. I could hear Roger in my ear telling me to calm down and breathe. Come up, acquire your target and terminate with extreme prejudice.

"Three!" I jumped up and Allbright was already standing. As soon as I got to my feet he started firing. I could see the shower of flames coming from the end of his gun against the dusky sky. I never flinched. I brought the attaché up at the same time I produced the little 45. I pulled up on the handle and felt the recoil. I watched the orange color spill from the front of the case. I caught one in my left shoulder. It felt like I was hit by a bat with a nail in it, I tossed the case and the empty mini-gun.

I dove forward and landed on top of my two Glocks, while Richard was reloading. I came up firing and walked the pattern right up one side of Richard and down the other emptying both guns, 14 rounds out of the .45 and 20 rounds out of the Nine. When the smoke cleared, I was leaning up against the limo. Richard was in several pieces and Mr. Akimura was alive and well. I started to slide down the side of the car and landed on my ass in the dirt an empty gun in each hand with the slides locked back. In a few minutes the swirl of dirt and the whine of a turbine filled the air. The guys had secured the area. MC was tending to my wounds and Pepper was standing over me like a mother hen.

Roger came over and knelt down in front of me. "How do you feel?"

"I'm GREAT, I think,"

"That's the morphine talking," MC offered.

"I have something for you." Roger took my hand and placed something cold and pointy in it.

"You deserve this. It was my honor to serve with you." He stood. MC stood next to him. Face, PQ, Aaron-Ben David and Pepper fell in right beside them and stood at attention. I opened my hand and held it near my face.

"Lt. Commander Rowdy Calhoun, it is my distinct honor and great pleasure along with the rest of your team and peers to present you with my Navy Budweiser making you an honorary member of our SeAL Team."

All hands saluted. The tears were running down my cheeks freely now. I saluted them back and they stood at ease. "It has been my privilege to serve with every one of you. Thank you for the piece of your lives you have all given to this mission." Pepper looked at me and winked.

"So which one of you disobeyed a direct order?" All hands took a step forward, Roger spoke "We decided to use Aaron as a sniper, figuring Richard would have no idea what he looked like, he rented a motor home and parked, taking up a position about a half mile from here" "what the hell did you use?"

"A .50 caliber Barrett, you know for when you want to reach out and kill someone"

MC and Face helped me to my feet and into the back of the limo with Mr. Akimura.

"Rowdy-San. Thank you for coming to get me."

"Hai, Doi Tashi Mas Te Akimura-Sama, it is my honor to be here today".

Christmas Eve had us escorting the Bennets to visit, husband, father, grandfather... Pepper and I stood at Chief Bennet's grave. Both of us in dress whites. My uniform had a new addition to it, a gold Budweiser. The girls, Janet and Sharon, along with Mrs. Bennet and Ruth, stood behind us. Pepper shouted, "Ten Hut!!! Officer on deck." We saluted the Chief whose memory will never perish from our thoughts and on this day had the chance to say our final good-byes. I spun on my heels and turned to embrace Mrs. Bennet. "He watches over you two you know."

"We know. We wouldn't have it any other way."

As I walked over towards Ruth to put my arms around her, it began to snow flurry, "its been a while since Riverside has seen snow", Mrs. Bennet said, "he knows your here".

"Take care of yourself and the kids. I'll be around if you need me, but only if it's an emergency." She was crying and nodded her head.

I walked over to Sharon and put an arm over her shoulder. "So, miss me?"

"Oh yeah. We have so much to talk about, including getting ready for a wedding." Her voice went up five octaves. I turned my head and looked at Pepper. He shrugged his shoulders.

"You were the one that told me once you find a girl to put up with your shit, marry her."

I extended my hand to Janet. She took it and we walked to the truck.

"You mad?" She raised an eyebrow.

"Now what would make you ask a question like that?'"

"Honey, I love you."

"I know. You always come home to me. I love you too!"

ABOUT THE AUTHOR

Andrew P. Cohen is a true renaissance man, in all forms of the word. A marketing and public relations professional who has devoted his life to the automotive aftermarket.

Born in New York in 1964, Cohen's passion for the automotive aftermarket shows in the specialty vehicles that he has conceptualized, designed and constructed along with the products & companies that he's promoted through the use of image vehicles.

Mr. Cohen splits his time between his homes and business in Arizona and California.

When he is not designing, fabricating, writing, producing or working directly with clients on private builds, Andrew can be found out in the desert pre running, sight seeing via motorcycle or carving corners in one of his custom built vehicles.

He is always contemplating his next business venture.

OFFENSIVE BEHAVIOR II

"Most people wake up on Christmas day to find gifts and good tidings under their tree. Not Rowdy, he wakes up to find Uncle Sam under his tree."

Sept 2001

The white lines start to become one as I move down the Texas highway, 80mph during the day and 65 at night, the carcass' that litter the side of the road tell the tale, hit a deer at speeds just under the century mark and there wont be a lot left of anything smaller than a full-size truck or SUV.

I'm on my way back from hunting some drug dealing scumbag who turned some rich Hollywood type's fifteen year old daughter into a heroin addict and party favor, he wanted justice in the form of his kid back and the aforementioned shitheel delivered in a black duffel bag and dropped at his feet. I wanted the pay that went with a gig that comes with kidnapping, torture and the extraction of a human (if that's what you would call him) from one country into another.

I led a team of newbies with the exception of my old partner Craig.

"I can't remember when we were that young"

I said to him as we got ready to cross the border after stashing our getaway Ford Excursion in the bushes and then covered it with camo nets.

"We weren't he chuckled, we were always older".

He flashed me a smile, clicked his com link and gave me a "check check", "I got you five by five", I threw my right hand in the air and did a circle motion letting the rest of the team know were ready.

The bank of the Rio Grande is pretty soggy and as I got closer to the swift moving water the dirt gave way and in I went up to my knee, "this is colder than I thought it would be", I whispered into the waterproof Bluetooth the guys at Cardo Systems designed for my team and I.

"Quit bitching and keep moving before we all sink up to our necks in this shit and have to call border patrol to rescue us" Craig scolded.

All of the sudden it was cold up to my waist, fuck me running I hate working with soggy drawers I thought keeping my complaints to myself. Craig and I heard it simultaneously the helo that homeland security uses to patrol the shallow river in this area looking for illegal's crossing into the US not really looking for a team of shooters heading the other way. I'm sure it would be a real bingo to catch us armed to the teeth looking like we are going to invade Mexico.

We all stopped dead and lowered down eye level with the cool water, we needed to mask our heat signature as the chopper team would be employing the latest in thermal imaging technology most likely a third gen Raytheon unit, we did not want to be caught so under the water we went. The green and white Hughes 500 hovered momentarily and moved on, we finished our crossing hunkered low to avoid detection and in under twenty minutes we were across the river and in another country.

I opened my dry bag and retrieved my Smartphone, powered it up and opened Google maps, I had previously loaded the coordinates to our destination and all we needed now was a large SUV or sedan, I spun around at the noise of a fast moving vehicle only to realize newbie-wan had already helped himself to a seventies era ford station wagon complete with rear facing jump seats that fold into the floor, if I had made reservations with Enterprise this is what I would have wanted.

"Not bad newbie" I said as I slid into the passenger front seat.

"Keep straight on this street for about three miles", I turned and looked at Craig who was texting his girlfriend telling her he was going to be home later and asked if she wanted to go to dinner, see a movie or just fuck like rabbits. She opted for the latter, my kind of girl I thought, "does she have a sister"? I asked.

Since Janet took off with the kids I find my nights rather lonely and since I like sex as much as the next guy it couldn't hurt to ask.

Craig tried marriage once but unlike me he learned his lesson and didn't repeat his mistake, I on the other hand was on the lookout for the future fourth ex- Mrs. Calhoun. He shook his head no but she does have a sex-crazed friend who is looking for something to do for the rest of the weekend before she leaves the country on Monday,

"Interested"? "Does the pope wear a funny hat"?

"Set it up and have her text me a pic and an address".

I might actually get lucky for the first time in months.

"Left here and then a quick right down the alley"

I pointed to the screen and newbie-wan nodded, he wheeled the car with the precision of a get a way driver leaving a bank that's just been robbed, I nodded in approval. He cut the lights and we glided down the alley when we got close he killed the engine and all I could hear was the crunching of dirt, broken glass and assorted trash under the bald tires.

Newbie-two had already disabled the interior light, which amazingly still worked after almost thirty years; they don't make cars like that anymore. The heavy car rolled to stop without the use of the brakes and NW quickly moved the gear selector from D to P in a smooth enough motion that I didn't feel the car come to a complete stop.

We bailed out quickly and took our positions, "maybe these kids know what the fuck they're doing", I thought to myself.

I had the front door, Craig had the back door and the newbie twins had to climb up and handle the second floor, the plan was to quickly and quietly grab the girl, said scumbag and retreat without firing a shot.

I guess the newbie twins forgot to read that part of the memo because once inside all hell broke loose and it sounded like world war three, fuck me running twice. That's just we need right now is the sound of gunfire on an otherwise quiet street, I'm sure the scumbag I've come to collect is at this very moment locking himself inside a safe room calling for reinforcements most likely in the form of the local bought and paid for policia.

Under normal circumstances I wouldn't have a problem taking on the local gendarmes however they have radios and are monitored by our friends at No Such Agency which does in fact talk to their friends the Christians In Action who talk to you guessed it, Homeland Security. FUCK, FUCK, FUCK!

I tsk tsked into my mike to get Craig's attention, I did not want to add to the loud noises if I didn't absolutely have to, as I thought that, I had to.

The first of several drug dealing shitbags came at me through a passageway between the kitchen and living room, I fired a three round burst from my MP5 taking him and several expensive looking china pieces behind him in the china cabinet, the second guy was ready and knew where I was firing from so he came in hot and fired directly at where I used to be, surprise asshole another three round burst and his head popped open looking like ripe melons all over the wall.

We were beyond being quiet now and yelled into my open channel for everyone to hear it time to end this little standoff and get our packages and GTFO.

Craig was engaged in hand to hand combat with two guys who came up behind him from a hidden door we weren't privy to, I could hear him grunting and groaning (I thought he was getting laid) amusingly fighting for your life and sex sound a lot alike. I came up on their little threesome and grabbed one guy by his hair pulling his head back stretching his neck so when I ran my Emerson along it from ear to ear it would be an easy slice both jugulars would fill his throat with warm sticky blood drowning him in seconds.

The other guy was Craig's problem, I had to find the newbies and possibly kill them my mood was slightly dour. I hiked up the stairs three at a time reaching the top and was immediately greeted by automatic gunfire, "they're down the hall with the head cheese and the girl" newbie-wan said.

"You two could fuck up a wet dream, I told you cocksuckers no shooting, WTF over"?

"We were shot at as soon as we got inside, it's like they were waiting for us" number two explained, "well now we have to advance through a hail of gunfire to get our intended targets and leave, Barney Fife and his minions will be here in under five minutes, so draw straws or compare dick sizes, I don't fuckin care how but one of you is going down that hall first"!

Craig finally joined the party and we took stock of ammo, I had six mags of thirty rounds left and he had eight, "jeezus fuck, don't you shoot anyone anymore"? I asked.

He smiled and produced his blade which was covered in blood.

"I'll lay down cover fire while you two idiots go down the hall, when those two pop they're heads out of the door way to shoot you, kill them, got it"?

Newbie-rella and his date staged and on my command ran down the hall while I sent sixty hot rounds down range over their heads, just as I predicted shitbag one and two popped out of the doorway and the twins displayed and overwhelming show of force and Craig and I ran down the hall to join the party, as I guessed the house did in fact have a safe room but only the door was hardened, so I punched a hole in the wall to prove a point, he unlocked the door and came our begging for his life offering us wealth and fame to not kill him.

Little did he know we weren't going to kill him, only deliver him for whatever fate awaited him so I really wasn't lying when I promised not to kill him and accepted his bribe.

The girl was strung out and needed a fix, unfortunately we had to give her one otherwise she wouldn't go quietly, so I mixed up enough to get her by and after removing the rubber band from her arm she collapsed and Craig tossed her over his shoulder and off we went, I could hear the sirens wailing getting closer, we missed them by twenty seconds a clean getaway.

The big Ford came to rest close to where we had to cross the river, the thought never crossed my mind the cold water could wake the girl, it had been a long time since seeing someone go through detox and the icy water would feel like a million needles puncturing her skin all at once, she snapped to about half way across and started screaming, newbie-wan thumped her and dropped down low in the water so as not to attract too much more attention.

We climbed out of the Rio Grande about a half click from the Excursion and humped it all the way, we could not risk exposure at this stage and I was concerned HS would do a low pass flyover and see us.

We made it to the SUV without further incident and headed home, I dropped the twins off in a Lowes parking lot in Murrieta, Craig and I headed to Hollywood Hills to drop of our cargo and get paid. We drove the two hours in silence, which was occasionally marred by the muffled groans of shitbag who was having a hard time breathing through the dirty sock I shoved in his mouth before Craig taped it shut. Our heroin princess was starting to come to so Craig gave her water, she fell back to sleep and stayed that way as we carried her up the stairs and into her fathers house.

Craig handed the girl off to a manservant looking gent and I dropped the scumbag at the feet of our employer as promised. He knelt down to unzip the bag and I put my size thirteen magnum boot on his hand preventing that from happening, he looked up at me and I waved my finger back and forth in a no fashion.

Mr. Hollywood stood up and I said, "two things, one, money. Two don't open the bag until we are gone, I don't care what you do to him but I don't want to be here when it happens".

He looked at the second manservant looking gent and nodded his head, the proper gentleman handed over a messenger bag, I unzipped it and peered inside, "it plus a bonus for bringing my daughter home alive".

I nodded and spun on my heels, Craig and I didn't even slow down as Jeeves opened the door and we went skipping down the stairs three at a time to the Ford, Craig backed down the driveway and in fifteen minutes were back on the freeway heading home.

"So, what's for dinner Craig asked"?

Fast forward, present, Christmas day.